In Case You Didn't Know

KAYE ROCKWELL

In Case You Didn't Know

Copyright © 2022 by Kaye'Rockwell

All rights reserved.

No part of this book may be reproduced in any form or by any electronic or mechanical means, including information storage and retrieval systems, without written permission from the author, except for the use of brief quotations in a book review.

To my husband, Thomas.

Thank you for saving my life then giving me one worth living.

To Lauren,
In case you Didn't know,
I'm Glad you Exist!

Skye.

Prologue

Noah

"Alessandria?"

Are my eyes playing tricks on me?

Am I so desperate to find her that I've conjured her?

Is she really here?

I'm unable to move, shocked at seeing her in the same room as me, let alone an aisle away.

Then the woman standing ten feet away from me stiffens.

I'm certain she's real.

She's in the middle of grabbing a box of pasta from the shelf when I call out that name. Pulling her arm back, she makes a show of reading the box before throwing it in the cart.

She's pretending she has no clue I'm talking to her.

She turns slightly, showing me her back as her elbows spread out on the handle of the cart.

My training kicks in and I track her every breath and movement.

She's in a defensive stance, shielding something in her cart

Positioning herself carefully, she hides her face from my line of sight.

Her feet shift, and there is a subtle change in the way she's standing.

She's about to run.

Why? Why is she so determined to run?

It's been a year.

Did it all mean nothing to her?

Did I mean anything to her?

Maybe she never really knew me at all.

"RIA."

I say it louder this time. Loud enough that I know she hears me clearly. Loud enough that she can't pretend she didn't hear me.

The set of her shoulders become more rigid.

Her movements are subtle, but I catch them. Not just because I'm trained to do so but because I know this woman better than I know myself.

I watch as she takes something out of the cart, carrying whatever it is close to her chest

She's taking it with her so she can bolt.

I won't let her. She owes me an explanation. A reason.

She owes us that much.

In my head, what once was confusion, heartbreak and borderline desperation turns into anger.

She's bolting.

She's running away from me, again.

But I won't let her not until she tells me why.

It's been over a year since I last saw her.

Since I last held her and kissed her.

I spent months trying to track her down, but I failed .

Until now.

Under the harsh fluorescent lighting of this small-town grocery store in the middle of Red Cloud, Nebraska.

I finally tracked down my wife.

Noah

Six Years ago.

I must be dreaming.

She's come around the bar. She's headed straight to me and with the way she keeps her gaze locked on mine, I know today's the day her curiosity has piqued.

She walks towards me in a cloud of determination.

My girl's got guts.

Shit.

She's not my girl. She's a girl. This girl has guts.

I need to remember that if I want to walk away from this interaction unscathed.

My heartbeat picks up and heat spreads through me like wildfire at the intensity she radiates with a single stare. Her eyes widen and I wonder if she feels this as much as I do.

Whatever this is. This almost tangible energy. This undeniable attraction that sizzles and pops in the distance between us.

Julia, another barista, calls out to her as they walk out the door. Disappointment builds then dissolves when she doesn't break our stare down. She simply raises her hand, waves, and calls to her. Without looking away.

Impressive.

Her mouth tilts up as she nears, and if I hadn't spent the

last three weeks watching her, I wouldn't be able to say that this smile she's fighting against is a real one.

It is.

"Hi there." She slides into the barstool next to mine, sipping on what smells like a strawberry tea as she leans sideways, her shoulder resting on the bar.

"Hey." I murmur letting the word roll off my tongue in a rumble.

I've only got three more weeks before I start at the FBI Academy and for the first time since I decided on this path at sixteen, I'm not looking forward to it.

I've been working towards this goal for the last seven years. It all started with the last foster home I ended up in. My foster father was a retired police officer and although he wasn't a pleasant man, those nights he spent spinning tales about his good ole days with a badge stuck with me. Though I suspected half of them were made up, after spending most of my life in and out of horrible foster homes, I welcomed the discipline and rules he provided.

What is it about her that is making me second guess myself?

Like a moth to a flame. I want to be near her. I think about her constantly.

Worry about her when I don't even know her.

For the last two years, I found myself drawn to this place. To her.

For the last two years, I got curious. It's in my nature. At the time, I refused to be deterred. I threw myself at my job and focused on my work. My job as a CSI was the stepping stone to a career I've been dreaming of. I couldn't afford any distractions. So, I stayed away. But I only succeeded in pretending. The second that job ended, I was supposed to pack up the studio I was renting and drive to Virginia to look for an apartment near the academy.

Instead, I found myself extending my lease for one more month. For reasons I didn't want to dive into, I stayed. I came on a random day and waited in the café like the awkward lonely teenager I used to be and I've come to realize I never really grew out of it.

I told myself if she was still here and I still felt that connection, then it meant there was something there.

Something worth figuring out.

There had to be a reason I was so drawn to her.

She says nothing, her eyes leave mine and drift towards my open laptop. I currently have the browser on searching apartments in Virginia.

The moment she sees it, her left eyebrow shoots up and she looks back at me.

Curiosity and a ton of questions swim in those gorgeous brown eyes. Up close, I can see the flecks of gold and amber in her seemingly milk chocolate-colored eyes.

A lock of jet-black hair falls on her face when a gust of wind follows someone entering the shop and I grab hold of my coffee just to keep my hands from reaching out to brush it away. With that comes a whiff of vanilla and roses, a scent utterly her own.

She shifts in her stool to face me entirely. Her knees brush my thigh. Though we're both wearing jeans, heat seeps through and I instantly ignite.

My grip tightens on my cup, and my control wavers, belying the years of training I've had.

Her cheeks turn pink letting me know she's not entirely unaware of the chemistry crackling between us. Whatever this is… it's not one-sided.

Dropping her now empty plastic cup on the counter, she rests her chin on one hand while extending the other. "I'm Ria."

"I know." I grasp her hand firmly in mine, relishing in the warmth of it against mine.

Ria's brow wrinkles and I grin at her, letting her hand go. I gesture towards her nametag.

"Oh!" The pink in her cheeks deepen and she lets out a laugh that has me zeroing in on the blush in her cheeks that now perfectly match the color of her mouth.

"I'm Noah."

She bites her lip and points at my coffee cup. "I know. I make your coffee." Or at least that's what I think she says. I'm too fixated on the way she's chewing on her bottom lip.

I know I'm about to tip the scales, and either this is the best decision I've ever made or this blows up in my face. But at this moment, I don't care. I've always played it safe. It's time I did something for myself not because I need to but because I want to. I want to get to know her.

I relax my shoulders and ease into the same position as her. I strategically place my left leg outside of hers and lean in close.

I give her my best grin and watch as she visibly swallows.

"Do you want to have dinner with me?"

Ria's breath shallows. I let myself appreciate the way her chest rises and falls before meeting her now widened eyes. "But I... You... I mean I..."

She's sputtering now. Probably wondering how she went from casually sitting next to me to being openly pursued or maybe it's overthinking on my part. I do lowkey feel like a stalker after being here three times a week for the last three weeks.

"I'm going about this the wrong way. I don't want you to feel like I'm pressuring you but I get the feeling you want to know why I'm always here, right?"

She looks away with hesitation, flicking a glance at my laptop.

"I'll tell you about that, too."

Ria tilts her head at me, unsure. "I don't know the first thing about you and I'm not sure I'm comfortable going out with someone I don't know."

Now it's my turn to raise an eyebrow at her.

"Then how will you ever get to know me?"

She grins. "You got me there. I am curious though."

"How about this?" I lean my arm closer to her, lowering my head so I can look her in the eyes.

"We can go to that restaurant next door, where you might feel safer with people who can easily recognize you."

"Okay. When?"

"Tonight is as good a time as any. I mean if you don't have other plans."

I rub a hand on my knee, feeling suddenly vulnerable.

"I don't but…" She looks down at her work clothes, her mouth pinching.

I'm about to tell her she looks great when her cellphone rings. She leans over to pull it out of her back pocket, shooting me an apologetic look. Her hair grazes my cheek, the smell and feel of it lending to my already unruly thoughts.

Ria's mouth flattens into a thin line as she checks the caller ID. Heaving a deep sigh, she answers it with a frown.

"Hey, Penny. What's up?"

She listens for a beat before she slams her hand so hard on the countertop, it attracts the attention of the barista working the bar and some of the customers in line. She looks up and feigns a smile, waving off her coworkers' questioning looks.

Looking down at her lap, she plants an elbow on the counter, leaning her forehead on her hand to shield herself from onlookers.

I can see the tension building on her shoulders and her grip tightening on her phone.

"What the hell, Penny?"

She sneers, keeping her voice low enough that only I can hear. The hand not holding her phone drops into her lap and curls into a fist.

"I don't care! I told you I don't trust him. I told you what he said to me. Get the key back!"

She shuts her eyes, but I can see her anxiety mounting with each word this Penny is saying.

The hand resting on her lap now visibly shakes. I give in to the urge and place mine on top of hers, squeezing it for support.

Her eyes fly open, and she squints up at me. My senses heighten as I spot the sheer terror in her eyes before she quickly looks away.

She suddenly jolts upright. "Are you serious? Penny? Penelope!"

She mumbles a curse under her breath as she throws her phone on the counter.

"Everything okay?"

She barks out a short laugh. "No." Blinking hard, she shoots me another look of apology and stands. "I'm sorry. I can't have dinner with you tonight. I have to leave."

I gently grab hold of her arm, standing with her.

"Whoa whoa whoa. First, don't apologize. Do what you need to do. Second, you look absolutely terrified so please tell me how I can help."

She looks like she's about to argue but something flashes in her face—some recollection that resigns her to accepting my help. "Just give me a sec."

She rushes back around the bar to the café's back area.

I shut my laptop, shoving it in my backpack. I'm tossing my coffee in the bin just as she's rushing back out. She waves a hasty goodbye to the other baristas, Missy and Ann, and crooks a finger for me to follow her out the door.

I stop her just as we're about to cross the back of the building.

"Ria."

Her jaw clenches as she looks up at me with tears pooling in her eyes.

"Can you tell me what's going on first?"

I take hold of her shoulders and squeeze gently.

Tipping her head back, she stares up at the sky. The sun is setting right now, basking her in orange hues. I've never been this close to her, but now I see the little things that make her Ria.

A small bald spot on her right eyebrow.

Tiny moles on her left eyelid and underneath it.

Her pert nose, crinkling as she searches the sky for answers.

From my vantage point, I see her friendly façade crumble. The smile she puts on fades away as quickly as the sun sets and day turns to night.

"My roommate has spontaneously decided to fly to Paris to visit her dad. She's leaving tonight but the thing is... her ex-boyfriend still has a key to our apartment."

My grip tightens around her shoulders, and I squeeze gently, silently urging her to go on.

"They've been on and off for a while now and I just get a bad feeling from him. I don't...don't trust him." She pulls her scrunchie out of her hair and runs a hand through her dark mane. "CJ, that's his name. He always stares at me whenever he's over, looking me up and down. Makes a point of licking his lips and dropping inappropriate comments when Penny isn't around to hear. And last week..."

A sudden rush of protectiveness washes over me as a chill runs down my spine, anticipating her next words.

"Last week?"

"Last week, when Penelope was asleep, he cornered me in the kitchen."

I let my hands fall off her, curling them into fists because I get a sense of where this is going.

"Did. That. Fucker. Touch. You."

"He grazed my..." She gestures to her breasts. "He played it off like it was an accident but then he said it didn't have to be an accident... if I knew what he meant. Then he boxed me in and told me to leave my bedroom door unlocked."

I grit my teeth.

I've heard enough.

A low growl rumbles in my throat. "So what's your plan?"

"Change the locks. Then I'm going to pack my stuff and go from there."

"Pack your stuff?"

Sighing, she gestures for me to follow her to her car. "My lease is up this month. Well... technically I don't have one. Penelope's mom owns the apartment and I pay her rent but as per our agreement, I'm only obligated to stay until the end of the month. After all this though, I think I'm just going to head out early. I never planned to stay here permanently anyway."

A shiver runs through me.

Do coincidences like this exist? Is this some sort of cosmic joke or is this really happening?

Her plans mirror my own.

I shake those thoughts and focus on Ria.

"So where do you go from here?"

She shrugs as she unlocks her car. "I don't know yet. I graduated last week and figured I had two more weeks to figure out where to go, but I was thinking D.C. since my advisor mentioned computer programming is a huge industry there."

My eye twitches. "Did you say D.C.?"

How is this possible?

"Yes. D.C. or New York, or honestly? Anywhere but here."

I shelve this information for later and focus on the more pressing problem first.

"There is a Lowe's in this complex. Do you know how to change locks?"

She shakes her head, looking anywhere but at me. I can tell she feels self-conscious about the way she just opened up to a total stranger.

"Alright. I'm parked near there. Do you feel safe enough with me that I can follow you home and help you out?" Pulling my wallet out, I hand her my driver's license and work badge. "Take pictures of those and send them to someone you trust so they know you're with me. I want you to feel safe with me and know that I'll protect you if it comes to that, alright?"

I've never been prouder than in this moment, taking in her widened eyes as she stares at my CSI badge, her fingers tracing the emblem of the local police department.

"You're a cop?" she asks, seemingly surprised.

I'm quite proud of what I've become, given I came from nothing. Even though the disbelief in her tone should put me off, it doesn't. I spent so much time at the café, maybe she doesn't believe I actually have a full time job, let alone wear a badge.

Hopefully, after all this is said and done, I'll have another opportunity to ask her out. Maybe out for coffee or lunch. I need to explain to her why she's seen so much of me these past few weeks.

I grin and shrug like it's nothing. "I'm a sworn officer of the law." I nod my head towards the hardware store at the other end of the complex. "Let's go."

Ria

He's a police officer.

The guy who has been coming in at every one of my shifts for the last few weeks is a cop.

I wonder if he knows that we know--that every single person who works at the café has noticed that he's only here when I'm on the schedule. I really should be creeped out, but everyone insists it's flattering.

Missy and Julia, who I work with the most, have sung his praises as they ogled him from the other side of the bar. I don't typically do friendships, but I've worked in this café with them for the last four years, so they're the closest thing I have to friends. If they think he's worth a shot, I feel sort of obligated to follow their advice. It's not at all because I also find myself intrigued by the guy... and find him somewhat attractive.

I bet none of my coworkers have ever spent a night in their pajamas watching true crime shows. It's always the good-looking guy who turns into a serial killer.

Hello, Ted Bundy.

Ironically, Noah sort of looks like Zac Efron.

The way his lips curled up and his eyebrow hitched up to his forehead like he was trying to figure me out? It made me feel seen. I may not know the exact moment things shifted

IN CASE YOU DIDN'T KNOW

for me, but I grew curious. I started wanting to figure him out.

Call it curiosity or mild attraction but today, I felt that push to approach him.

It didn't seem like he was ever going to make a move, so it appeared safe for me to be friendly. Then he asked me out.

He really asked me out. And I really said yes. Until, of course, Penelope had to ruin it.

That girl must have some internal radar so she can sabotage me whenever something good happens. As crazy as that sounds, I wouldn't put it past her. Ever since I could remember, she's had a vendetta against me.

Our moms were friends once. Growing up, I know they had both hoped that somehow we would be friends too, but that never happened.

We were way too different, and she simply hated me on sight.

Penelope does what Penelope wants--living the life of an entitled rich girl.

Aunt Patty has come to terms with it over the years, but I think she still hoped I could knock some sense into her daughter but it never shifted from the initial animosity, I was never able to fix our relationship. She hated me through and through.

After my mom died and Aunt Patty offered her condo, I jumped at the opportunity.

Living with Penelope has been a chore and ironically enough she doesn't do a single one. Early on, I had to put my foot down and make her switch rooms with me because I got sick of cleaning the bathroom just for her friends to dirty it up when they were over. After the third time I found coke lines on my sink and had to air out the smell of weed, I gave her an ultimatum: either she would give me privacy and hire a housekeeper to do her chores or I would tell her mom. I didn't know how she would react given that she and Aunt Patty were pretty close, but to my surprise, Penelope agreed. Probably too afraid of getting cut off from the purse strings. She definitely needed the money to keep up with her lavish lifestyle. In the years that I had become her roommate, I quickly realized that she was as entitled and spoiled as could be. She was constantly partying, and when she wasn't, she was shopping. The third bedroom in the condo was specifically allocated to her as a second closet, filled with racks and stacks of clothing and shoes.

I couldn't fathom living the way she did. I may pay Aunt Patty close to nothing for a place to stay but I still did my part in making sure I respected her and was grateful for what she's done for me. Thanks to her, I've been able to save money for the last few years.

Enough that I can get the hell out of here now that I've got my diploma.

I'm no stranger to the nomad life. I even prefer it.

The condo building comes into view, and I quickly tap on the breaks to signal Noah, who's following me in his car..

Noah.

He is still very much a mystery to me. He asked me out only after I approached him which makes me think that he was never going to make the move. Making me even more curious and confused as to what his motives were for hanging around so much.

I park at my designated spot and point Noah over to where the visitor parking is.

I grab my things, including the Lowe's bag that has all the things needed to change a lock.

Thank God he came with me because there are things in life that I can do but changing locks is not one of them. I wait by my car as he gets out of his.

He scans the area quickly as he strides across the parking lot.

"You good?"

I take note of the cautious way he takes in his surroundings without it becoming too obvious as he continues his way to me. When he repeats his question as he comes to a stop in front of me, still alert but his eyebrows knit as though he's genuinely concerned, it takes every amount of self-preservation I've built up over the years not to shiver at the low rumble of his deep voice.

At a distance, I've acknowledged he is one good looking man. But up close? It's nearly impossible not to get caught up in those blues, the color of the sky with his smile radiating the same warmth as a spring day. The way he stares at me like he can see right to my soul. It takes everything in me not to combust when he directs all that masculine energy my way and acts like I'm the only person in the room.

Then a small gust of wind sends his scent my way. It reminds me of the cedarwood candles my mom loved. I restrain myself from leaning over and having a whiff.

What if I actually sniffed his neck? Not that I can reach it but still…

I'm definitely feeling some attraction to this man. Pheromones? I think that's the word.

"Ria?"

I blink the errant thoughts away, realizing he must have called my name a few times and I never actually responded to him.

I nod, clumsily hoisting my heavy purse on my shoulder as I lead him to the elevators. Heat rushes through me when he slides my bag off and carries it for me without a word.

I flush, and a slow knowing smile spreads on his face.

"So, tell me about this guy. I want to be able to spot him."

He leans a shoulder on the wall adjacent to the elevators

as his eyes continue to sweep the parking lot. If anyone walked by right now, they'd think he was simply having a conversation with me instead of actually being on high alert. How have I never noticed it before? The way he's always so carefully aware of everything and everyone around him. How, from this close, he has this whole alpha protector thing going on and damn if it doesn't make me feel safe.

A feeling I'm not familiar with.

"He's big and burly. A little bit taller than you, maybe six-five? He has blonde hair that's always in a greasy ponytail. Tattoos up and down his arms. One arm is covered in female cartoon characters." I choke on a laugh, remembering the first time I met him and how he thought I was admiring his tattoos but really, I was trying not to laugh. CJ reveled in the whole macho thing he had going on so the fact that he had cartoon figures that were created to objectify women inked on his skin is hilariously on brand for him. "Like Betty Boop and Jessica Rabbit. And on the other is just a bunch of squiggly lines that I think are Celtic symbols? But he also has guns on that side... like a rifle with some sort of tag?"

He raises an eyebrow but stays silent as he follows me into the elevator, his eyes still trained to the parking lot like he's expecting CJ to appear out of nowhere.

When the doors close, I shut my eyes and rest my head on the wall. We're standing on opposite ends of the elevator. I can feel his eyes on me but the stress of the last week has gotten to me. After I told Penelope what her boyfriend said to me, she didn't believe me until CJ made the mistake of asking her to invite me to a threesome.

She broke up with him, acting like I had been secretly trying to steal him from her. On top of finals, graduation and my impending move... I've never felt so tired and alone.

"You're not alone in this, you know. I've got you."

IN CASE YOU DIDN'T KNOW

My eyes flutter open but I keep them lowered as I stare down at my boots.

How did he know what I was thinking?

"I don't even know you."

His low chuckle echoes through the small space we're in.

"Noah Thomas. Twenty-five years old. I've lived in Whatcom County for almost three years and before that, I lived in DC. I'm a Crime Scene Investigator. I spent most of my time here in Washington working with the Bellingham Police Department. Anything else you want to know, just ask. I may not know you well either but I do know you deserve to feel safe. I'll make sure you never feel unsafe again. I promise you that."

My mouth falls open at his candor. Our eyes meet and I feel something bloom inside of me.

Something I haven't felt since my mom died.

Hope.

He takes a small step towards me, his eyes full of heat and promise but before he can do anything, the elevator dings and the doors open to my floor.

I shake myself out of the trance and lead him to the end of the hallway and my door.

I unlock it, letting him in. I'm about to shut the door behind him when he stops me.

"Go ahead and change. Shower if you want to or whatever you usually do after work to unwind. Let me take care of the locks."

He gently peels the plastic bag full of tools and the new lock from my fingers, shooing me away. He gets down on his knees by the door and starts taking the stuff out. I remain standing there, paralyzed for a few moments as he gets to work unscrewing the old lock from the hatch.

When he raises his head to smile at me, I return it and

head to my room to shower and change, feeling safer than I have ever felt in my life.

I'M fresh out of the shower and wrapping my cardigan tight around my body when I hear a loud knock coming from the front door that quickly turns into erratic pounding. I run to the living room and find Noah leaning on the back of the couch, glaring at the door with his legs crossed by the ankles. He tips his head to the door and motions for me to stand next to him.

"I'm going to open the door but just follow my lead, okay?"

Just as I open my mouth to ask him what he means, I hear CJ's voice booming from the other side of the door.

"ALESSANDRIA. OPEN UP. IT'S ME."

Unwittingly, I take a step back. My arms fold themselves at my waist and a shiver runs through me. It was only a theory that he would come back, knowing Penelope would be gone.

He actually showed up.

"Ria."

Noah's eyes come into focus, and I realize he's bending down to meet my eyes. His hand gently cups my face. "Don't be scared, sweetheart. I got you. Just follow my lead, okay?"

I nod then jump in surprise when CJ goes from pounding to kicking the door.

Noah's eyes turn murderous, a dark storm clouding his blue eyes. Straightening, he heads to the door, yanking it open but keeping his body aligned with mine in a clear protective stance as he shields me from the intruder.

"What the hell do you think you're doing?" Noah doesn't yell. His voice is even but it's the clear, no-nonsense tone that he uses that shows he is not one to be trifled with.

"WHO THE HELL ARE YOU?"

CJ's head moves around to see behind Noah. His eyes flick around the room until he spots me. He tries to force himself inside the room, thinking Noah will balk and let him but Noah stays fixed.

"I believe I asked you first. What are you doing trying to break in?"

"BREAK IN?" CJ starts to laugh but something in Noah's eyes makes the laughter die in his throat. "I have a key," he says through clenched teeth.

Noah laughs. "If you did, you wouldn't be pounding, kicking and yelling for the door to be opened. So my question is, once again, what are you doing?"

CJ openly stares at me, daring me to disagree. "I'm Ria's friend. I came by to see her."

"Is that true, baby?"

It takes me a split second to realize Noah is addressing me.

Right, this must be my cue to follow his lead.

I straighten my shoulders and stand at my full height, which is not much but the message is clear. He will not scare me.

"Absolutely not. He's not my friend and he's definitely not supposed to have a key."

CJ's mouth pinches at my response.

Noah cocks his hip, leaning on the doorframe.

"Do you know trespassing is a criminal offense in the state of Washington? And if found guilty, you can be charged with a gross misdemeanor or a class B felony depending on the charges?"

"What the fuck?! Who are you?"

CJ's eyes bounce between Noah and me.

Rolling his shoulders back, Noah shifts ever so slightly to where I can see his profile.

Not so subtly, Noah's hand flicks down to the bottom of his pullover sweater to show his badge that now hangs from his jean pocket.

With a smirk, he nods my way.

"I'm the guy who's going to arrest you for trying to break into his girlfriend's apartment."

Girlfriend.

Okay, I know.... I know Noah is putting on a show for CJ's benefit, but his use of the word has my heart skipping a beat. I've never had anyone address me in that way but somehow, hearing it come from Noah doesn't feel strange or wrong.

CJ's eyes widen as he takes in Noah's badge. Then the words start to slowly sink in.

"I-I didn't know she had a boyfriend, man." His hands go up and he takes a step back. "Seriously bro, she's been throwing herself at me and I swear the key worked last week. I thought, you know, I'd check on her. Make sure she's alright. You understand right, bro?"

Noah's entire demeanor changes at CJ's choice of words. No longer is he the calm, totally in control man he was two seconds ago. Noah's jaw hardens as he pushes off the doorframe. CJ might have a few inches and pounds on him, but CJ looks completely shaken.

Noah's legs are parted in both a protective and possessive stance as he braces his arms on the door and its frame. I can no longer see what his face looks like, but I can tell by the way CJ is practically shaking in fear that it's not pleasant.

"So here's what's going to happen. First, you're going to apologize to my girl. Second, you're going to commit this moment to memory. I'm giving you one free pass here. Don't waste it. If you ever come within one hundred feet of Ria or even think of pulling this shit with another woman ever again, I will hunt you down. Trust me when I say this:

you do not want that. Because next time, *bro,* you'll be begging for that misdemeanor. And by then, it'll be too late," Noah barks at CJ, his voice practically dripping with acid.

He makes a show of pulling his phone out and taking a picture of CJ. He tosses me a pointed look over his shoulder as he slides it back in his back pocket.

"I'll be right back, baby. I'm just going to throw the trash out."

CJ mutters a curse then takes a decisive step back. "I can see myself out. Ria, I'm sorry."

With that, CJ huffs as he speed walks around the corner and out of sight.

I collapse on the couch, hand over my heart as I shake my head at Noah in astonishment.

He was nothing short of brilliant. It was like watching a scene out of Chicago PD. I can't believe how quickly he diffused the situation without escalating it.

Noah takes his phone out, quickly tapping something on it before settling on the couch with me. Our couch is one of those sectional couches that can fit four people in it. He's careful not to invade my space and sits on the L end of it.

Clearing my throat, I offer him a grateful smile. "Thank you."

One side of his mouth quirks up as if fighting his own. Clasping his phone in his hands, forearms resting on his knees, he leans forward. He seems to consider how to respond.

Suddenly, I'm nervous to hear what he has to say. He went above and beyond for me tonight. Regardless of whether he does have some weird fascination with me, he did more than necessary. He kept his promise to protect me and make me feel safe.

I feel a twinge in my chest, a poke and a prod. My heartbeat speeds up and the temperature climbs at least ten degrees between us.

Whatever this feeling is, it's intense and shoots straight to my core.

I've never felt like this before.

Like an emotional cocktail of happy, worried and content.

And honestly, kind of turned on. I resist the urge to fan myself.

It's all because of this man sitting three feet away from me.

A man I barely know.

A man who has been coming to my place of work with the sole intention of seeing me.

"Ria." He addresses me almost cautiously, his voice just a bit louder than a whisper.

Pulling my knees up and resting my back on the arm of the couch, I turn to face him.

I remain silent as I wait for him to say his piece.

"Are you okay? Do you feel safe?"

"Yes, I do. You kept your promise."

Noah turns to look at me, a grin forming on his handsome face.

"Good. I'm glad." He expels a breath. "No one does that to you and gets away with it."

Placing his phone face up in between us, he taps the screen to show me.

"I ordered food while you were in the shower. I saw a menu sitting on the kitchen counter and figured it would be my best bet in getting you something to eat that you like though I'm not too familiar with Filipino food. It should be here soon. I promised you dinner." He winks at me. "I intend to keep all my promises to you."

Not wanting to get into it quite yet, I scoot closer to get a good look at his phone, beaming at him.

He ordered the hapunan, which consists of all my favorites: sinigang, lumpia and adobo fried rice. Perfect for the chilly weather and for dealing with the aftermath of what just happened.

"Great choice. I hope you like sour soup, vegetable rolls and fried rice," I muse.

Tipping his head he says, "So you like it?" A hopeful smile passes his lips.

I roll my eyes. "You managed to choose three of my favorites, stalker."

My eyes widen at the slip of the tongue.

I reach out and grab his arm when his face mirrors my shock.

"I am so sorry. I didn't mean that."

He shakes his head, squeezing the back of his neck. "No. No, it's okay. I guess after weeks of seeing me so often. You could assume that. I mean, you should assume that."

Shaking his head again, more profusely this time, he holds a hand up and squeezes his eyes shut.

"Shit. This isn't coming out right. Can–can I explain?"

Letting go of his arm, I lean back. "Please do."

"I was curious."

"Curious?"

"Curious of the girl behind the sad smile."

His eyes meet mine. Something in them begs me to stay quiet and wait for him to continue.

"It was two years ago. I saw you crying in the back lot. Then I watched as you pulled yourself together and forced yourself to smile... to go on. I was in awe of the sheer will it took to get you there. For the last two years, I've wondered about you. Wondered if you were okay. Wondered what made you so sad. I couldn't bring myself to go back because I knew if I did, I wouldn't be able to pull myself away. Something kept pulling me back to you however because the second I quit my job, I found myself back at the café again. That first day, I saw you fly around with a smile that didn't quite reach your eyes, yet you managed to fool everyone. I never meant to make you feel uneasy or unsafe with my presence. But just like the coffee, it was addicting. I found myself needing to see you. To make sure you were alright."

My hand flies to cover my mouth as I listen to him describe one of the worst days of my life. The day I had to pack up the apartment I lived in with Mom. She died just the week before and that same day, I was told by our landlord I had to leave. I packed what I could into Mom's car, storing it in the cheapest storage facility I could find, and then I drove to work knowing that was it. That was the end of living and the beginning of surviving.

"My mom died two years ago," The words tumbled out of me in a rush.

I search his eyes, taking in his reaction. He looks taken aback for a second then his eyes soften in understanding. It encourages me to keep going.

"That day you saw me? It was a week after she had passed. My mom's medical expenses had piled up. Even after I dropped out and was working three jobs, I was still struggling to pay our bills on time. By the time she died, I was already a few months behind on rent and I got evicted that day. I packed up what I could, dumped it in storage then went to work like nothing had ever happened because I had no other choice but to keep going."

Noah shifts so his body is angled towards me, letting me know I have his full attention. I can't help but marvel at the fact that this man cares enough to listen to what I have to say.

"How did you end up living here?"

"I ran into Aunt Patty at one of my old jobs at a retail store. I had no idea she and Penny had moved here as well so when she offered me a place to stay, I took it. And as luck would have it, shortly after that, I was contacted by a nonprofit that offered to pay off the rest of mom's hospital bills."

"That must have been such a relief."

I nod, sinking into the cushions. "It really was. For the first time, I didn't have to worry about money and just be. I enrolled myself back in school and now here I am."

"What about your dad?"

My eyes drop to my lap. I should have anticipated this question. After living my whole life not knowing who my father is, you would think I would be numb to his nonexistence but the mere mention of him still hurts.

"I never met him. All my mom would tell me was that she met him on one of her trips to the Philippines."

The only person I have ever opened up to like this was my mom. The fact that I'm here with Noah right now, talking about my life is making me feel self conscious.

"You're incredible Ria."

I bite my lip, unsure how to respond.

"I'm serious, Ria. You've gone through so much on your own. Your strength and resilience is admirable."

I simply stare at him in awe. I'm unsure about a lot of things and I've never felt worthy of anyone's kindness. It was a rarity in my life that's only happened a handful of times so it's unfamiliar. Uncomfortable even.

But this time, it's different. It isn't any of those things.

After a few moments of me just staring at him, he starts to fidget nervously in his seat, worry creasing his forehead.

"Are you mad? I can go... I think I should probably stay the night, but if you don't feel safe with me here after what I just told you, I'll sit in my car and make sure he doesn't come back."

I have no idea what I've done in my life to deserve someone like Noah and I don't know if I deserve it either.

But I'm exhausted.

I'm tired of being alone.

Tired of having to pretend I'm not breaking inside.

I'm tired of being scared.

Maybe it's time to live like my mom.

She always saw the good in people.

She never let horrible people or terrible moments make her stop believing.

I've been living my life guarded and controlled for so long.

It's time for a change.

It's time to take that leap of faith Mom always preached about.

"Stay. Please stay."

With that, I grab the remote from the coffee table and hand it to him.

"As long as you don't pick any scaries, I'll let you choose our binge."

The smile I get in return chases my worries away, leaving goosebumps in their wake.

Noah

After a few minutes of bantering about our tv show preferences, we ended up binging a police procedural she loves while we ate our dinner and she questioned me about the authenticity of the show. I tried my damnedest not to burst her bubble because of the way she kept shooting me hopeful looks. As if I would ever tell her that the show doesn't even begin to compare to the real thing.

She drew me in with the way her eyes welled up anytime one of the characters got riled up to the way they lit up at the 'gotcha' moments. Somehow, I felt like she was letting me be privy to the Ria no one else got to know. Every single time she laughed or angrily shook her finger at the tv, I felt myself fall a little bit more. These little moments she shared with me felt like a gift.

Halfway through the third episode, she turns to me.

Ria tucks her hair behind her ear, and just like that I'm once again struck by how beautiful she is.

"What about you? Where are your parents?"

"I never knew them. I was raised in foster homes until I was eighteen."

"Tell me about them."

I pause, unsure how much to divulge. Ria had a crappy night and is finally smiling. I didn't want to dampen the mood.

She reaches over and covers my hand that's resting on the back of the couch with hers.

"Please?" She gives me a half smile, her eyes shining with a soft kindness, I've begun to associate with her.

"There's not much to tell honestly. After a while it got repetitive," I chuckle, humorlessly. "I got stuck in homes with fosters who could care less about the kids in their home and cared more about the checks they were cashing in."

She doesn't say anything, instead giving me a supportive squeeze with her hand. The warmth of it urges me to continue. I've never shared any of this with anyone but in this moment, with her looking at me like that, I'd tell her anything.

"I've seen some really bad stuff, Ria. I've been with foster dads who abuse, foster moms that hit and sometimes I even ended up with foster parents who didn't even bother to feed me or let me bathe because they were too busy using the money to do drugs than to actually care for the kid they took in. Eventually a neighbor takes pity, or a social worker comes to do a random check and I end up getting pulled out of the home and into another... but that shit stayed with me. I knew then that I never wanted to end up like them. I didn't want whatever crappy card I'd been dealt with to dictate the rest of my life."

She sniffs and a tear slides down her cheek. I sit up, feeling guilty for having made her tear up but she stills me with a gentle pat to my hand.

"Did any of them... ever hurt you?"

I give her a stiff nod and when her eyes widen in horror, I do my best to muster up my most reassuring smile. "I've been cussed at, had things thrown at my head and a few times, my arm was pulled a bit, but I've always been able to defend myself, so it never got too far. Over time, I've learned to stay quiet and make myself scarce around the homes. As long as I had a roof over my head, food in my belly and I was able to go to school, I was good. Eventually I ended up with this retired marine who had recently lost his wife. His daughter had encouraged him to foster so he wouldn't be lonely and though it wasn't the best home I'd been in, it wasn't the worst. I learned discipline there. I found my calling there."

She smiles again, her knuckles coming up to brush her tears away.

"This may sound weird but I'm in awe of you, Noah. You managed to turn your life around into something quite remarkable. You should be proud of yourself."

Noah

I had spent most of my life alone and don't remember the last time I wasn't.

Last night with her looking at me the way she did, with no sign of pity and telling me I should be proud of myself, it stirred up feelings I didn't know I was even capable of.

I felt a sense of camaraderie with her. She made me feel hopeful and yes, damn proud of myself even more than I already am.

I told her how I wondered if that's why I kept gravitating towards her. Because I saw a soul akin to mine. A kindred spirit.

Her eyes had widened, then her lips curled in a soft smile but her eyes started drifting at this point, and with a mixture of disappointment and amazement I noticed that it was well past midnight.

We had spent hours alternating between watching her show and talking.

As I watched her finally succumb to sleep on the couch next to me, I also realized this is the most fun I've ever had with anyone.

That knowledge echoes and ping pongs all around my head through the night. Bits and pieces of our conversation crawl their way into my subconscious, filling my dreams.

I fall asleep not long after, only to wake up to a pan clanging on the stovetop.

I hear the distinct sound of Ria muttering to herself.

I stifle the urge to laugh but the smell of bacon and something garlic-y permeates the air, causing my stomach to make an unintelligible sound. Coupled with a full bladder, I have no excuse to lie here and eavesdrop on her one-sided conversation with the frying pan.

"Good morning! I can hear your stomach growling from over here."

Grinning, I sit up to find that she had covered me up in a blanket at some point last night.

"I hope you're not a vegetarian... because then I'd have to respectfully and politely ask you to leave so I can eat my bacon free from judgment."

"Definitely not."

Chuckling, I turn my head to greet her and words fail me.

I've never woken up to a woman before.

The women I fall into bed with never spend the night and I never stay over either.

I mentally pat myself in the back for that choice. I doubt any of them would hold a candle to Ria.

I'm aware my mouth is slightly open and I'm staring unabashedly at her, but all I want is to drink in the sight of her.

The curtains that adorned the walls last night have been pulled to each side of the wall. It's now adjacent to the floor to ceiling windows that surround the living room and dining areas giving a clear view of the city below. But despite what I'm sure is a spectacular view, I'm hypnotized by the even better one of Ria.

Her hair is braided off to the side and she's wearing a white dress that falls just above her feet making her look like an angel coupled with the sun streaming through basking her in a glow.

And don't get me started on all the tantalizing skin showing just below her collarbone.

Cautiously, she sets the bowl of rice down on the table as she stares back at me.

I shake my head at her and muster up a smile as I let my eyes wander back to the windows then to the spread she has laid out on the table.

She eyes my movements as I ease off the couch.

I fold the blanket quickly over the armrest and meet her by the table.

She's not wearing any shoes so the difference in our height is more evident as I stand next to her. She purses her lips as she tilts her head back to peer up at me.

I look down at her, seeing her bare toes peeking out from under her white dress and her face devoid of makeup.

I've never been this close to her.

This feels intimate somehow.

I avert my eyes before they stray too long anywhere. I have only ever seen her in long sleeved shirts so all this skin is doing odd things to my stomach.

I've never felt this intensely about someone before. For as long as I can remember, I've kept to myself. Even in foster homes that were not so bad, I never let myself get too close to anyone.

But I have this need. This urge to be close to her.

Like a moth to a flame. I'm attracted to her light.

Yet it's her darkness that calls to me the strongest, so familiar to me.

The sadness in her soul calls to mine.

I'm desperate to know all the things that make her smile and chase her demons away, soaking up as much of that sadness away, so she never has to fake a smile again.

"You cooked breakfast?"

Her smile is slow and I watch it grow on her face in fascination.

"I realized when I woke up this morning that I never

thanked you for helping me out last night." She turns to go back to the kitchen. "And for staying the night when I'm sure you had better things to do."

"Pretty sure those plans involved you too."

Ria looks over her shoulder at me and for a moment I bask in the awe in her eyes.

It's a thing of beauty, the revelations flashing through. Like she can't believe I'm real or that anyone could possibly do something as simple as ensure her safety.

"Believe it." The words slip before I can catch them.

Her eyes expand to saucers and she turns back around to face me, a dish in her hands.

Smelling as delicious as she looks, I can't bring myself to look away.

Why her?

Why me?

Why now?

There's a reason this thing between us is so strong, so palpable in its intensity.

For the first time in my life, I find myself wanting someone, needing someone.

But then I watch as her eyes dip to her feet, breaking the connection between us, and I take a mental step back.

For now.

I incline my head towards her room. She had let me use her bathroom last night, but I still wanted her permission knowing everything is always different in the morning.

I don't know where her head is at but I know she feels this between us.

And she's scared.

"Do you mind if I use your bathroom?"

Her eyes meet mine again shyly. "Yes, of course. I set a toothbrush for you by the sink."

. . .

IT DOESN'T TAKE LONG for me to wash up. I shuck my sweater off, leaving me in the long sleeved shirt I had on underneath. I run my fingers through my hair as best I can as I leave her bathroom.

I'm trying to win the girl here, not scare her off even more with this nest on my head.

I pause inside her bedroom for a moment.

It's like she doesn't even live here, the space completely devoid of personality.

It's sparse except for a small shelf of books on her bedside table with a few personal items and a single framed photo.

Because curiosity is in my nature, I pick it up.

It's a picture of a young couple. The woman, who I'm guessing is Ria's mom, is the spitting image of her except for the eyes. No, those eyes clearly belong to the man in the photo.

This must be Ria's father.

I set the picture back down, my eyes sweeping across the room once again.

There's a suitcase sitting inside her open closet with clothes folded in it and a few hung.

The only other sign of her is the bed, comfortable with its pale blue sheets, comforter with a Sherpa blanket that looks like it's well loved and two decorative pillows.

I stare at the bed longer than I should and heave a deep sigh.

Her room looks exactly like mine-- like a hotel room. Temporary.

Tossing my sweater over my shoulder, I walk out of her room and back towards the dining area just in time to hear her curse and a cupboard slam.

I bite back a smile.

Ria isn't a morning person.

What I find back in the kitchen stops me in my tracks.

Then I'm practically vaulting over the bar top separating the dining and kitchen areas to get to her faster. She's on her knees on the countertops trying to reach the top shelf. Her arms are shaking, and her position is unsteady.

My hands go to her hips to prevent her from falling and she tumbles back with a startled gasp.

I wrap my arms around her instinctively, cradling her back on my chest.

"Are you okay?"

"I-I needed a mug."

Fear lodges in my throat. I acted on instinct. The thought of her falling off the counter and onto the marble floor and hurting herself was too much for me to bear.

I can feel myself shake just by the mere thought of it.

Ria trembles in my arms.

I feel her every breath.

Her scent wraps itself around me, filling me with a toe-curling need stronger than anything I've felt before.

My hands tighten around her and I breathe her in, trying to will myself back to reality.

We're practically strangers and there is no way I'm going to pressure this woman in my arms to do anything she doesn't want to do.

Not until she's ready.

Not until we've figured out what exactly this is between us and how we'll move forward.

But then she turns her head to look at me and I see the same need reflecting back at me. Something inside me grabs hold and I know this is it. This is the moment in my life I'm going to look back at, wondering what if I didn't take this chance being handed to me.

I've never wanted something--someone more in my life. I ache for her.

When her gaze falls from my eyes to my lips and back again, I give in.

I turn her in my arms before setting her on the counter. My eyes lock with hers.

I lean in, bracing my hands on either side of her.

"Can I kiss you?"

My voice comes out raw and needy but I don't give a damn. I want her.

I need her.

She slowly nods her head as she visibly swallows, her eyes trailing back down to my lips.

I don't know who moves in first but we come together instantaneously.

Her hands curl around my shirt as mine fist in her hair.

The same need filters into this first kiss, then the next and the next.

We ravish each other.

Our breaths mingle as we take huge gulps of air before coming back together.

Hands searching each other, learning and exploring.

Until I forget where I end and she begins.

It's new.

It's messy.

It's raw.

It's everything.

Her legs part then wrap around my hips, pulling me in, and I'm a goner.

My forehead touches hers.

"Tell--tell me what you want. I'll give you anything, Ria." I rasp at her, my control slipping.

Her fingers trail a path up my chest to my jaw and my eyes flutter open to find hers.

"You."

It's a whisper. Her eyes are wide with her confession but

she doesn't break eye contact this time as her fingers trail back to my neck.

My breath hitches at the intensity in her eyes and I groan as I smooth my hands down her back to lift her against me.

I chase the errant thoughts of this being too soon to the back of my head.

I'm only hanging on to the certainty I feel of having her in my arms.

It feels good.

It feels *right*.

I carry her to her room and lay her on the bed, aligning my body with hers and I ask her one more time.

"Are you sure?" I cup her face gently, kissing the tip of her nose.

"Are you?"

"Baby, I've never wanted anything more in my life. Never wanted anyone like this before."

Ria searches my eyes for a moment.

The moment might be two seconds that stretch into minutes, hours, or years in my mind.

My need for her consumes me and I watch for her next move with bated breath.

Her hands go to the straps of her dress, and she unties the knots before pulling me down on her.

She kisses me more fervently this time, whereas before she was searching, learning, giving in to lust.

This time it's with resolve.

Raw fucking need.

"Noah?"

Her lips dance on mine and I have to force my eyes back open.

I find her smiling at me. "I'm sure."

I know with every fiber of my being that when I have her, nothing else will matter.

That thought should scare me, but it doesn't.

With a sharp tug, I pull my shirt off and kiss her again.

I show her just how badly I want her.

Because fuck--now that I have her, I'm not letting go.

I WAKE up just in time to see her slip out the door. I give her a minute.

And then another.

Then I get up, pull on my jeans and follow her out.

Ria is sitting on the carpeted floor. She has her arms wrapped around her legs, her chin resting on her knees as she looks out the large windows.

She's so deep in thought, she doesn't even notice me.

I clear my throat and wait for her to look up.

"Hey."

A deep sigh escapes her as she looks up at me.

"Hey..."

I run a shaky hand through my hair, a heavy feeling in the pit of my stomach.

Regret. That is what I think I'm seeing right now.

It would gut me if she said she regretted it but I ask her anyway.

"Do you regret what we did?"

Her head shoots up and she shakes it so adamantly I'm afraid she's going to pull a muscle in her neck.

"No, I don't."

"Then what's wrong?"

She rests her chin back on her knees, her gaze flitting back to the window.

She pats the spot next to her, inviting me to join her.

She waits for me to sit before she says anything.

"I'm scared, Noah. And confused." Her eyes bounce everywhere but me. "I'm not sure what to think about any of this."

I join her in staring out the window.

"I'm scared too, Ria but I'm not confused. I *like* you." A short laugh escapes me. "Fuck that. I more than like you. I *care* about you."

"You don't even know me."

I reach over and grasp her hand, tugging her gently to look at me.

"I know you, Ria. Maybe not the little things that make you, you but I know what matters. You are kind, patient, hardworking, generous and," I grasp her chin, "—fucking gorgeous inside and out. You've seen some bad shit in life and yet you still choose to be a good person."

Her chin trembles and I kiss her forehead. My hands move to cradle her cheeks.

"You know what else I see when I look at you?"

She shakes her head, pulling at her bottom lip with her teeth.

"I see a woman I want to get to know even more. A woman I want to call mine if she'll have me. I may be scared that this is all moving so fast but I'm not confused. The second I laid eyes on you, my soul--my soul knew you."

"Noah—"

"I'm serious, Ria."

She shakes her head again but this time she pulls away, tears pooling in those chocolate eyes.

"How-how can you?"

I let my hands fall helplessly to my side, in frustration.

Because how the fuck do I explain this gut feeling? I don't know anything other than the fact that she calls to me somehow. I'm pulled to her in a way that I can't ignore.

"I don't know."

She shuts her eyes, inadvertently shutting me out.

"Ria."

My fingers move on their own accord, wiping her tears as they spill down her cheeks.

"Do you feel anything for me?"

Her eyes fly open and I see it before she confirms it. The emotions swimming in her eyes.

"Yes but—".

"But nothing. What do you feel, Ria?"

"I—". She turns to look away but I capture her cheek gently with my palm, urging her to look back at me.

I want to look her in the eyes when she tells me this.

"I like you too. I don't know how and I don't know when it happened but I do."

I nod, but I remain silent, sensing she needs to get more off her chest.

"This isn't me. You have to realize that. I don't sleep with men I just met. I don't even date. Yet I'm sitting here in your shirt, and I fell asleep in your arms. It's all too much, too soon."

She starts to shake with emotion as her tears continue to fall. I can almost taste her fear.

The emotions playing out in her face are akin to mine. Familiar.

She's scared of how good it feels between us.

Scared she's not good enough.

I hold my palms out, and she places her hands in mine.

"Are you leaving?"

I nod. I am. I was.

All I know is I can't leave here without her.

"So are you."

"You have a plan."

Again, I nod.

I told her about the Academy last night.

"What are you really scared of Ria?"

Her lids lower. "You have plans, Noah. Plans that don't

include me. Yes, we're both leaving this place but unlike you, I don't have a plan. I don't know where I'm going or even what I'm doing with my life. You have your whole life mapped out."

"Pretty sure my plans also included you."

Her brows meet in uncertainty.

I uttered those words to her earlier but this time I mean them in a different way.

"Ria. Doesn't it feel like we were always supposed to be in each other's plans?"

She opens her mouth and I place a finger on her lips.

"How else do you explain this pull between us? The fact that we met each other like this. That of all the coffee shops in Seattle, I stumbled upon one you worked at? Or that we're both leaving this place?"

"I don't know."

"I do. There's something here, Ria."

"What are you saying? That I should leave here with you? We've barely known each other for a day. We can't just move across the country and live together."

"That's not what I'm saying."

"Then what?"

"If you want to live in D.C., Virginia is not that far away. I'll drive to you. Every free moment I have will be yours. Do you think I'm like this with just anyone? I prefer to be alone. I like my solitude. I've never even been in a relationship. But with you, I'm willing to give it everything I've got. You make me want things I never thought I deserved. Give us a chance, Ria."

She takes in my words and I revel once again in the emotions playing on her face.

She was always a mirage to me. The lonely girl with the fake smile.

Now she's real. She's here.

She's not hiding anything behind a smile.

"I don't even know where to begin." She trails off as she picks at the hem of my shirt that falls short on her thighs and I have to peel my eyes away from temptation.

"Earlier... when I asked you if you were sure and you said yes. Where is that certainty?"

She shrugs, her vulnerability calling out to me. I want so desperately to take care of this woman. To finally give her that safety and security she's been missing.

"Earlier, I wasn't thinking as much as just feeling, you know? I've never felt this way either, Noah. I don't want you to think it's all you because it isn't. It's just––I don't... I don't know."

I suppress the urge to take her in my arms.

I don't know if she even knows she's looking at me with so much hope, her eyes dancing all over me as my words wrap her in a hug she so desperately wants to ask me for.

"If I had to hazard a guess it's because you've always operated alone. You've been burned in the past and it's hard for you to trust that this is real and I won't leave you?"

Shock registers in her face at how attuned I am to her thoughts.

She can only nod her head, her eyes bouncing between mine.

"I feel the same way Ria. I've had my whole life planned out and then suddenly I see you and I can't stop thinking about you. Now that I know how easy we just fall together? Not just in the little things but in everything."

"Everything?" Her voice comes out in a shaky whisper, like she's both afraid and needing to hear me spell it out for her.

"Everything," I assure her.

I scoop her onto my lap, tilting her face up so we're inches apart.

"Even with the fear that my shitty life has instilled in me, there is no way I can just walk away."

I see everything in those eyes. I see a future.

For the first time in my life, I feel hope and a certainty that almost steals my breath.

Like my soul recognizes its other half in hers.

"Ria. We may have only shared hours of conversation but in that short time, you bared your soul to me like I did with you. I told you things I've never shared with anyone else. You trusted me with your body which you admitted isn't easy for you. Before you, there was only the weight of my baggage holding me down. Now I could float to the fucking moon with how light and good you make me feel, baby."

I kiss her forehead and my nose trails a path to her hair to breathe her in.

I allow myself a few more seconds to get lost in her scent and feel before I set her back down on the floor and rise.

I grab the sweater I flung on the table when I hurried to catch her earlier and pull it on.

There's not a lot more I can say to convince her without pressuring her.

As much as I care about her and as much as I wish I could make her say yes, this is her decision to make. It's not mine to force.

"I'm scared for all the reasons you are, but I know if I don't at least let you know, I'll regret it for the rest of my life. Ria, I'm not going to pressure you. I want you to make the decision that's best for you. Just know that you have me if you'll have me. If you decide to take this chance with me, I'll support you. In case you still couldn't tell, I'm crazy about you."

I grab my keys and phone from the couch where I left them and pocket them.

In the corner of my eyes, I see Ria stumble to her feet.

"Where are you going?"

I force myself to give her a small smile, shoving my hands in my pockets.

"I don't want to push you, Ria. All this is crazy and new and terrifying for me too. We're both so used to being alone that I have a feeling we'll go around in circles if we don't hit pause. I'm giving you space to think about what you want."

Her fingers curl into small fists at her side and I can tell she's fighting the urge to make me stay knowing I'm right.

We need space. I need to take a step back and think too.

I never intended to do any of this--none of this was part of my plan.

Yesterday when I was at the café, I never thought she would approach me.

I was on my way out when she did and the series of events that led to this moment right here opened my eyes to the possibility of us.

I need to think about what life with her would mean to the plans I had for myself. Training at the academy will take up a lot of my time.

Will she be willing to be with someone she barely saw?

What happens after and I'm assigned a job that isn't in Virginia?

Would she move again to be with me?

I run my fingers through my hair in an effort to calm the nerves bubbling inside me.

Ria stares at me with so many questions in her eyes that I wish I had the answers to but all I can think about is the fact that I'm handing my heart to a perfect stranger hoping she atleast hands me back a little trust in return.

I run a shaky hand through my hair, waiting for her to speak. I feel like I've run a marathon with how much pressure I feel against my chest.

"What now?"

I shrug noncommittally, spotting a sticky note on the counter with a pen next to it.

I scribble my number on it quickly.

"Now we give each other space. I'm going to go back home and finish packing. I'll be around until Friday before I have to go. I'll leave my number here. If you decide you'll have me, just give me a call or even a text. I will be at your door the second you do. If you don't, you can toss my number in the trash and I'll assume you've decided it's not worth the risk. Even if you don't want me, I still want you to have someone to lean on in case of an emergency. I swear I'm not pushing you Ria, but I do care about you and I know if I stay here longer, I'm going to want to do things. I need to go while I still can."

She takes a moment, folding into herself as her arms go around her middle. Then with a deep sigh, she nods and looks down at her feet.

"What about your shirt?"

Fuck it.

I cross the room back to her, tipping her chin up as I gaze down at this woman I want more than I've wanted anything, and that includes a stable job at the bureau.

I drink in the sight of her, my gut churning with uncertainty.

"Keep it. If this is the last time I see you, I want to remember you this way."

Ria

It's been two days since Noah left and he's supposed to be leaving tomorrow.

I sit on the edge of my bed as I stare at my packed bags and once again mull over what I should do. I worked my last shift at the café last night, hoping the closure will help me make up my mind. All night I wondered if he would show up and for the first time in weeks, he never did.

I guess he meant it when he said he wouldn't push me.

I flop backwards on my bed just as a text comes through my phone and I almost break my neck as I jump to grab it from underneath my purse.

It's just a text from Aunt Patty confirming she booked a moving company for me.

I called her after Noah left and let her know I changed the locks and had no choice but to tell her why. Penny didn't even let her know she was flying to Paris, let alone that she was seeing anyone. Aunt Patty apologized profusely. Then she offered to have my car and my things in the storage unit shipped to wherever I decide to move.

For the first time in my life, I didn't feel the need to feel guilty about taking her money and readily agreed.

Still, there's no text from Noah.

Then I groan when I stupidly realize I never gave him my number.

For a man who practically made his presence my shadow for three weeks, he sure knows how to make an exit.

I miss him.

He's right. Even though we only talked for a few hours, it solidified what I already felt--

an attraction and connection unlike any other.

It wasn't instant for me like it was for him. It was a culmination of a few things.

He may have thought he was the only one watching me but I was watching him too.

In those moments when he had his head buried in a book or his focus was on his laptop, my attention was zeroed in on him.

That's when my attraction started growing. In the tiny smiles and brow furrows as he immersed himself in a book and how he was genuinely kind to the other customers at the café.

I watched as he held doors open, talking to the older patrons and playing with the little kids. I loved the way he could hold conversations with anyone at the café.

I miss his presence that felt like it would take up the room and now, his absence that nearly pierces my soul.

Everything about those moments we spent together, just the two of us, felt like a preview to a life I've always wanted but never felt I deserved. I feel like for the first time in my life, there is actually someone out there who wants to be with me, take care of me and maybe even love me the way I so desperately ache for.

I rub my chest where a pang hits me again. I can't forget the look in his eyes as he bared his soul and laid his heart out for me. The way he graciously walked away so I could figure it out, made me feel like what I wanted mattered. He didn't force his hand or give ultimatums. Even my mom forced me to do things. And yet here was a guy who wanted it to be my choice, regardless of how he felt.

What the fuck am I still doing here?

I grab my phone, hastily swinging my purse around me as I rush to the door.

Then I realize I don't have his number saved.

I scrounge around my purse for the sticky note as I open the door and that's when I notice I'm not alone. There's a person standing on the other side of the door.

"Ria."

I suck in a breath as I look up to find Noah standing there, his blue eyes piercing mine with restrained emotion.

"Noah... What are you—how are you—how long have you been standing there?"

His hand clings to the doorjamb as his eyes wash over me.

He's drinking in the sight of me like a man dying of thirst.

"Awhile." He releases a breath as if he had been holding it in painfully. "I'm sorry, Ria. I know I said I'd wait, but I just had to see you again."

I shake my head furiously at him because words are failing me right now.

There's a meteor sized lump forming in my throat and my eyes are welling with tears.

It's like I conjured him up just when I so desperately wanted to see him again.

He seems to take my response as a rejection. He hangs his head in resignation and starts backing away.

I catch his hand as it leaves the door and tug on it. His eyes fly back to me, hope barely on the surface... but it's there.

This is all new to me and I don't know how to properly express myself, so I keep tugging on his hand until his body is halfway through my door and then I jump.

My purse hits him on the hip, but he barely flinches as he catches me.

His eyes are boring into mine, full of questions but he doesn't voice it aloud.

He simply carries me into the apartment, his face lighting up with amusement. He kicks the door closed, one hand around my waist as he uses the other to take the phone and my purse off me.

He drops them on the carpeted floor while he continues to gaze at me with slight curiosity.

My arms go around his neck as I'm afraid I'll fall if I don't hang on tight. He chuckles, adjusting me so my legs are now firmly around his waist while his arms wrap tighter around mine.

"Trust me, Ria. The last thing I want is for you to fall. Unless you know—." He grins and winks as he leans my back against the wall and we're chest to chest. He rests his forehead on mine, his eyes twinkling with mischief. "—you were falling for me."

My smile is slow when it comes but I don't doubt my feelings. Not anymore.

"Too late." My arms go limp as I let my fingers trail down until my hands are settled against his chest. "I already fell for you."

"Fuck." Noah breathes, his voice crackling with emotion. "Can I kiss you? Please tell me I can kiss you, baby."

I don't answer. Instead, I press my body against his and kiss him with promise.

After a few moments of the best kiss of my life, I whisper against his lips.

"Thank you for catching me."

"Until the ends of the earth, Ria. I'll always be there to catch you."

Ria

Present time.

Noah Thomas.
　　My ex husband.
Why is he here?

Why, after all this time, does he decide now is the time for him to show up?

And in the middle of a grocery store?

Is this why they finally let me go out? Because they knew he would be here?

I may not get a say in how I live my life or where but I should get a say in this.

He doesn't deserve my time and he sure as fuck does not deserve to see Adrian.

Not after all this time.

I scan my surroundings. Regardless of the *whys*, I need to remember the *where*.

We are in the middle of a store in broad daylight. There could be a threat anywhere.

We aren't safe and the most important thing to me is to make sure Adrian is safe.

Especially from the man standing ten feet behind me, piercing my back with his stare.

I unlock Adrian's buckle, careful not to jostle him as he

continues to gnaw on his teether. He's peering up at me and I have to blink back the tears at how much he looks like his dad.

I can feel Noah shift behind me like he's preparing to chase me down, just like he always said he would.

Just another line-- another lie he fed me for years.

I pick up Adrian, cradling him against my chest. I try not to startle him so he doesn't cry and we don't make a scene, but I need to get out of here. I want out of here.

I have no desire to see, let alone talk to my ex-husband.

Out of the corner of my eye, I see movement and I know one of the agents is getting in position to grab my cart once I signal that I'm done picking out my items. I'm nowhere near done but I'm not going to get another chance to go out. This is it. Or was it before Noah showed up and ruined our only chance to get out of the prison they forced Adrian and me in for the last year.

Trying to calm the rage pouring out of me, I make my move.

And that's when I see Gabriel Reyes. He's standing at the end of the aisle, breathless but somehow still in control in front of me.

His eyes flit behind me and his jaw tightens. He flicks his eyes around, lifting his shoulder in what appears to be some sort of signal. I hear Noah mutter a curse behind me but he continues to advance towards me.

I'm spared from witnessing whatever exchange they get into when Agent To, the female agent assigned to me, hooks an arm around mine and talks animatedly about flowers as though we're the best of friends. Seemingly undercover as a housewife from the nonsense she's spewing about gardening, she walks me out into the backend of the parking lot where a Ford Explorer waits for us.

I barely get Adrian seated in his car seat before the car

drives off in hurry with Agent Walker behind the wheel. Behind me, Agent To crawls to the back. She's sitting on her knees, her weapon drawn and she's scanning the area as we pass it with urgency.

What is going on?

Noah

WHAT THE FUCK?

I stifle the urge to make a scene and break my partner's face as I watch an agent, whose name I do not even know, practically drags my wife away.

Gabe repositions himself in front of me, so I still don't get a good look at what Ria is holding against her chest. My gut is churning and I have this feeling gnawing inside me that I know exactly what she's hiding.

Gabe's eyes flick over quickly to my left and I spot another agent with a cart walking down the aisle we're in. As quick and quiet as a mouse like the Academy has taught us, this agent leaves his cart and takes Ria's. Gabe grabs the cart left behind and walks over to me, a fake smile plastered on his face.

His eyes convey what doesn't need to be said.

We're undercover.

Play along.

"I only got to make two more stops at this 'ere place, man, then let's head on out before the missus starts ringin' and gabs about how I'm takin' too dang long to get her shit."

His fake Southern accent would throw me off if I hadn't heard him use it on one of our past cases.

I nod my head because God knows what would come out of my mouth if I speak now.

Clearly, my supposed best friend, my partner *and* the best man at my wedding knew where my wife was all along.

And from the looks of it, orchestrated the whole damn thing.

I'm going to let this play out until we're in the car but then I'm done playing this game.

I want answers.

Then I want to see my wife.

Fuck everything else.

Ria

I'm laying Adrian down in his crib when I hear a car door slam and footsteps pound on the gravel as the sound drifts into the cabin. I hear the distinct rumble of Gabe's voice right behind my door not even a minute later and then a heavy thud echoes through the crack under the door

I check that Adrian is still asleep and position myself in front of my dresser, my hand behind my back, ready to grab the Glock I have stashed in my nightstand.

The door whips open and I see Noah standing in the doorway, eyes wide and staring at me.

His chest is heaving and his hands are curled into fists at his side. There's a patch of blood on his chin that looks like it dripped from his cut lip.

That's when I spot Gabe on the floor behind him, being helped up by Agent Walker.

My hand instinctively dives into the drawer to grab the Glock.

Noah's eyes narrow at me. My hand starts to shake but I grip the gun tight in one hand as I shift to stand protectively in front of the crib.

I don't know what the hell is going on but my only focus is on protecting my son.

"Are you going to shoot me, Ree?"

My throat tightens, constricting at his use of the nickname my mom called me when I was a kid. Noah started calling me by that name shortly after I told him about it.

How dare he call me that?

My hand gripping the gun raises itself and points it at him. I stare at him in indignation.

I don't owe him a damn thing.

I want him gone out of my life *now*.

Again.

But as usual, Noah does what he wants and steps into my room.

His eyes trail behind me to Adrian and I swear he shakes with rage. Pain shooting out of his eyes as he stares at our sleeping baby.

Gabe follows him in, his hand reaching out to shove Noah back out.

"Man, let's not do this here. The kid is sleeping."

What can only be construed as a roar spills out of Noah as he shoves Gabe against the wall, an arm locking him in a chokehold.

"TELL HER. Tell her, you fucking asshole. Tell her what you just told me. Tell my wife what you did."

That's when I snap.

I shove the gun back into the drawer. With the way I'm feeling right now, I could kill them with my bare hands. The last thing I want is for my seven-month-old son to wake up and witness his own father's demise at the hands of his mother.

"I'm not your wife." I grab the baby monitor off the changing table and I storm out the door, knowing they'll follow me out.

I'm counting on them to follow me out because this is not a conversation I want to have in the same room my son is sleeping in.

I pass the spare room where they let me set up Adrian's

play area. I spot Agent Walker in the other room that's set up as their office looking over surveillance and Agent To in the room the agents sleep in, cleaning her gun.

I place the monitor on the kitchen counter, bracing my palms on the cool surface and attempt to take in deep breaths. My anxiety has been out of control since I found out I was pregnant, but it's even more unpredictable postpartum. Add that to the stress of being on forced house arrest by my ex-husband who didn't even bother to show up when I found out I was pregnant or even when I gave birth, my emotions are undoubtedly all over the place.

Then suddenly he's here, a month after I asked Gabe to serve him divorce papers.

What is going on?

I am so angry and heartbroken and sad and fucking pissed. I don't know what to do with myself.

I watch as Noah stalks in front of me on the other side of the counter and as he levels a dark look at Gabe who follows closely behind.

Something isn't adding up. Noah is pissed too. No, scratch that. He's livid. I have never seen him act this way.

And Gabe? He looks guilty... of what I don't know.

Gabe looks at me with a smile that doesn't quite reach his eyes.

Sadness mars his expression, and his eyes convey an apology.

"Ria, I need you to sit down before I start. I don't want you fainting on me or having a panic attack. We already risked way too much bringing you and Adrian out today. We can't risk bringing in paramedics here too."

Heavy breathing fills the air and I can feel Noah on the edge of a breakdown.

"Adrian? The baby is named Adrian?"

My eyes fly to Noah's of their own accord and just like

that, all the light and feeling missing from my life comes flooding back when our eyes meet. The numbness fades away and the knife that found itself lodged in my heart cuts deeper as I feel every inch of the pain and fear I had been shoving aside.

Noah trembles and braces his hands over the counter as though he's stopping himself from reaching over to me. His eyes fill with tears and he's shaking with every breath.

We do this for a few minutes, simply staring at each other.

Fifteen months.

That's how long it's been since I've seen him.

Yet the impact of his eyes still leaves me breathless.

He was it for me-- the one person I thought would never betray or leave me.

But here I am, a single mother, an ex-wife forced into hiding because of a case he was working on.

He put me here.

I was pregnant. Alone. Parenting. Alone.

And he has the audacity to waltz back in my life like he had no part in my isolation?

"Ria?" Gabe's quiet words break the spell Noah and I created in the room.

I falter for a second. I had forgotten that Gabe was even there.

I nod and make my way to the loveseat overlooking the lake and forest behind this cabin I've been living in for over a year. I keep my eyes trained on the view, not wanting to break down from the sight of Noah and steeling myself for what Gabe is about to say.

From the corner of my eye, I see Gabe walking around the counter to stand on the opposite side of the room. Noah stays in the kitchen.

Because of the open design of the cabin, somehow we're all still in the same room together.

"Spit it out, Gabriel." Noah growls and I spare my ex a quick look over my shoulder.

His head is hung low, a lock of hair falling on to his forehead, but his eyes remain locked on me, as though he's afraid I'm going to disappear.

Cerulean eyes, cherry lips, and chestnut hair.

I want to weep at the sight of him.

I missed him, despite my best efforts.

But unfortunately, I have spent way too much time crying over him.

All I can do is keep this stoic mask on, pretending I'm okay when I'm not.

Gabe takes a deep breath. "Ria. I am so sorry. I really hope you can understand why I had to do what I did. I hope you and Noah can forgive me someday. I only did this because I care about you both and it was the only way I knew how to keep you both safe."

"Stop shooting shit Reyes. Tell her what you just told me."

Noah's rage is almost palpable now as he shoves off the counter and his jaw tightens. He looks seconds away from unleashing his fury with his fists.

I see Agent Walker position himself at the doorway, possibly to get in between the two men should they find themselves in another scuffle.

I can feel everyone's eyes on me but I'm stuck on what Gabe is trying to say.

I feel my own anger rise, not even knowing the reason why yet.

"I lied." Gabe shakes his head, eyes shut. "About everything. Noah had no clue you were here."

My breath stills, coming out in a painful gasp.

He can't possibly be saying what I think he's saying.

"Two years ago, when we received intel that there might be a mole in the bureau and specifically in our team, Noah was one of the suspects. He was the lead agent in our investigation and when he was assigned the case, information started leaking. Knowing Noah, I was sure it couldn't be him but I couldn't give him a heads up. Instead, I had both your names planted in our servers to flag any correspondence and intercept a possible threat in an attempt to clear his name."

Gabe starts pacing back and forth, a hand shoving through his hair.

"That day I came to your house? There was a text message that was flagged in the system with your name, address, and picture, Ria. A single message came with it."

"What?" I breathe out, not wanting but needing to know.

"Get the girl. Kill the agent."

I shoot to my feet and my stomach plummets.

"I knew I had to get you out of there, but there was protocol I had to follow. I wasn't the only one who saw the flagged message. The director saw it too. Within an hour, he had arranged a safe house and transport to get you out. But under one condition: Noah couldn't know. He was still under suspicion and deep undercover at the assignment. Then when I got to your house, you were frantic. You were crying and begging me to call Noah, but I couldn't do that without going against orders and putting Noah and you in more danger. The only thing I could do was to lie, to get you out of that house. I told you he knew—that he orchestrated the whole thing. When I told you to write that letter saying you were leaving, it was for Noah's benefit as much as it was for whoever was going to come into your house."

The note.

The fake one I was told to address to Noah, where I wrote that I was leaving him.

My breaths come in gulps and I have to sit back down to ease the panic building.

Before I can even blink, Noah crosses the room to me. He kneels and places his hands on mine.

The heat of his touch burns and I rip my hands out from under his. He falls back like I've struck him and I struggle to make sense of the guilt I feel at causing him that pain.

I'm *supposed* to be angry with him, right?

I ignore Noah's tearful gaze as I look back at Gabe to continue.

"Then when we got here and you said you were pregnant, things had escalated in our investigation. Noah was cleared but we were still struggling to find out who it was in our team that was feeding Sotnas and his cartel with intel. We couldn't pull him without alerting whoever it was and we knew that if Noah found out you were pregnant, he would—"

I'm shaking my head in a desperate attempt to understand all this.

"Leave the job and come find me?"

Gabe sighs. "Yes. But that would put you in even more danger, so I made the decision to keep lying to you. To both of you. I told you he knew but he had a job to do. And I only pretended to help Noah find you."

Noah jumps to his feet and starts towards Gabe.

Agent Walker places himself between them, a hand to Noah's chest.

"Easy, Agent Thomas. Let's not do that again."

"Fuck you! All of you!"

"Noah…" It's a mere whisper but he hears it. His eyes lock with mine. His face is wet with tears and his eyes dance around my face like a mad man. "I want to hear the rest of it."

Gabe takes a half step towards me and I know what he's going to say before he even does.

"I fed him fake leads about where you could be Ria. Noah didn't know you were pregnant. He didn't know about Adrian until today. He did not abandon you. He never stopped looking for you."

I bury my face in my hands. I'm rocking with the gravity and the realization that Noah's job did this to us. Separated us. Robbed him of a chance to be with his pregnant wife and son.

I'm struck with the hardest realization of all.

And I believed them.

"Does this also mean we're still married?" I look up at Gabe, my voice an unsteady whisper.

"What does that mean?" Noah pushes Walker off of him and kneels in front of me again. "Why are you asking that?"

But I'm staring at Gabe because I'm not letting him get off easy.

Gabe nods his head once and I can tell he feels the weight of his betrayal.

"I know you asked me to serve him papers but you were under the impression he had done all this to you. I couldn't do that to Noah or to you. I couldn't do more damage to your marriage than I already have. I was still hoping we could wrap this case up soon, catch Sotnas and get you out of here before Adrian turns one. But when it wasn't looking like that was going to happen, I gave you fake papers and told you everything was done so you would stop asking questions. I wanted you to stop fixating on the notion that Noah abandoned you when that was the furthest thing from the truth."

I reach over and grab hold of Noah's shoulder to keep him from leaping to his feet again as he rages and spits out a string of curse words.

"That makes absolutely no fucking sense!" Noah roars.

I don't blame him. I'm about ready to throw hands myself.

Gabe knew.

He knew how hard the pregnancy had been for me.

How hard giving birth alone was for me.

How much I needed Noah yet he watched us both suffer.

And Noah? How could he not have known?

They were best friends. Partners.

Worked at the same company under the same damn boss.

How could he not have known they took me?

"I'm going to fucking kill you, Reyes. In case you can't tell, you're already dead to me."

This time, I let Noah go.

He stumbles to his feet.

I continue to sit dumbstruck, watching as my ex––my *husband* lunges at Gabe.

I'm helpless to do anything, still reeling from all of it.

Noah continues to stagger towards Gabe, and Agent Walker yells for Agent To's assistance to stop Noah from completely pummeling Gabe to the ground.

Gabe lets Noah take him by the collar, penance for his lies, for stolen time, for all of this.

A screeching wail comes out of the baby monitor, the telltale sign Adrian is up. I don't even spare anyone else a glance before heading straight to my room.

I shut the door, leaning against it. I allow myself a minute to calm my racing heart and take deep breaths before forcing myself to smile at my son.

Adrian's beady eyes and gums greet me as he continues to wail from his crib.

I pick him up, cradling him against my chest as I check to see if his diaper is full.

I go through the motions of changing him and put him in a new onesie. I'm only half aware of the yells and things crashing from the other room.

When Adrian's breathing gets steadier, I set him down in

his playpen and let him play with his toys. I turn on the sound machine to calming ocean sounds to drown out the noise coming from the living room. I forego the chair to sit on the floor, trying to distract myself with the sight of my son playing.

After a few minutes, things quiet down and I hear the unmistakable sound of Noah's footsteps outside the door.

He's careful about it this time. The door opens slowly but I don't dare look that way.

"Ria..."

I shake my head, refusing to look his way, but I feel his presence behind me. Then, before I can voice my refusal, I feel his warm body against mine. His arms come around me until he's holding me against his chest. Rocking me as I tremble with emotion, covering my mouth with both hands to keep myself from screaming, I sag against him and break down in sobs.

I don't want to scare Adrian but I'm scared myself.

I don't know how to separate the truth from the lies I was fed for over a year.

Even knowing the truth now doesn't erase the fifteen months of loneliness, fear, anger and pain.

I'm still mad as hell at Noah. But now I'm mad at myself too.

For believing that my husband could leave me like that with or without cause.

I allowed those lies to shape and destroy what I once felt for Noah.

I don't know what to feel about Noah now, besides disappointment and resentment.

I don't know why I'm letting him hold me like this when I am so angry at him.

"Fuck baby, I missed you so damn much." He buries his face in my neck, breathing me in.

I feel the heat of his tears and the press of his warm lips against my skin.

His voice cracks with emotion as he weeps with me.

He whispers apologies into my ear.

Once again, I forget where he ends and I start.

I let him hold me, but I don't touch him. My hands grip the hem of my shirt.

After a few minutes of him rocking me, Adrian starts to get squeamish, he must sense my distress so I pull myself together.

I lean away from Noah, waiting until his arms fall to his sides.

I still don't dare meet his eyes.

I'm not quite ready for whatever reunion he thinks this is going to be.

I push off of the floor, grabbing a face towel from the changing table to dry my face, tossing it in the hamper before I pick Adrian up.

Then it hits me.

Noah.

Adrian.

I turn Adrian enough so his dad can get a good look at him but keep my gaze averted.

This is all too much for me, but I need to keep it together.

For my son.

For his dad.

They deserve this moment, having been robbed of way too much already.

Silent tears stream down my face as I listen to my husband introduce himself to his son.

A son who is the spitting image of him.

Noah

Cerulean eyes, cherry lips, and chestnut hair.

I use the words Ria once used to describe me.

This kid.

My kid.

My son.

He looks exactly like me.

Fuck.

My eyes won't stop leaking. I'm sweating everywhere. I'm still shaking from the betrayal--from the realization that they stole my wife. My life. And now my son.

My family was taken from me. We were ripped apart by circumstances that were beyond my control. They hid them from me. For what?

Because I was working a case and they targeted her because of me?

I have an inkling there is more to this than Gabe has disclosed, and I intend to find out.

Something about the text he mentioned has been gnawing in the back of my mind.

And someone definitely orchestrated me finding Ria today. I feel it in my gut.

But first, I need to make peace with how much time I lost with my son.

"Hi-hey son…" My voice cuts off as gravel fills my throat

and I have to clear it to continue. "It's me. Your daddy. I'm-ah-I'm sorry I haven't been by to see you but I'm here now, okay?"

I choke on that last word. My chest heaves with the weight of everything I missed.

Ria still refuses to look at me and I know that even though Gabe pretty much absolved me of all imaginary crimes, Ria still carries that pain with her.

The abandonment, betrayal and heartbreak the bureau's lies have caused will take forever to erase from her mind and heart.

But Ria is it for me.

She's my other half—my soulmate.

She's everything and then some.

My soul only answers to hers and my heart only knows her.

I refuse to give up when it comes to her and to us.

And now, knowing we have Adrian, there is no way I'm going to stop trying to get her to forgive me for not finding her quicker. For letting her go through all of this by herself.

I'm not even sure if I forgive myself for not knowing something was off, or believing she would ever leave me in the first place.

But I'm here now and fuck if I'm going anywhere.

Ria

It's been over a week since Noah found us.

He hasn't pushed to have any conversations, instead spending the time getting to know his son. He asks me for permission before he takes Adrian every time, as though he's not Adrian's dad.

He feeds and changes him, puts him down for a nap and sleeps in the recliner chair beside the crib. I still don't have it in me to offer a spot on my bed and he knows not to ask.

He lives out of a suitcase that appeared that same night he found us and somehow got Gabe to procure supplies for Adrian and me.

I don't know how he managed that when it's been a headache getting the bureau to bring me anything other than my son's necessities.

Now, Adrian has everything a baby could want, including a closet full of new clothes and a playroom full of toys.

It seems like Noah is trying to prove himself by spoiling our son.

Like he can make it up to me by spoiling me. I look around my room at the candles, essential oils, diffuser and a shelf full of books that also showed up this week.

He hasn't said more than a handful of sentences to me except when he orders me to rest and relax. This is usually accompanied by him directing me to the bed and lighting a candle.

He then leaves the room with Adrian, and they spend hours in the playroom.

I've also noticed the agents that used to alternate guarding the outside of the cabin have been dismissed and only Agents Walker, To and Gabe are permitted in the cabin.

They moved their workspace to the basement, relegating what used to be the surveillance room to another bedroom. The three are now apparently permanently assigned here and only come up when it's time for meals or switch out for night duty.

Gabe attempted to apologize to me yesterday again but one look from Noah and he sighed, leaving to go do whatever it is they're doing down there.

I'm tempted to ask where they are with their investigation.

But at the same time, I'm scared to find out if they're close to getting this Sotnas guy.

Because then what? What do I do when I finally get out of here?

I can tell Noah is itching for us to be a family again, but do I want that?

He and Adrian will always be family. They're blood.

But Noah and I? I don't know how to separate myself from the reality I've been living in for fifteen months. The scariest thing is that I don't know if I will ever be able to go back to the person I used to be before all this happened-- to the person hopelessly in love with her husband.

I don't know her anymore. She floats in my head like a figment of my imagination.

Would I even remember what it's like to live a life that isn't in hiding anymore?

How will I support my son? Where will we live?

I know Noah will insist we live with him but I don't know if I want that anymore.

How do I fall back in love with someone who, regardless if he did it unknowingly, destroyed my life? I lost any sense of safety when I got locked away here, forced to fend for myself yet again.

Forced to stay alive for my son when every day I felt like giving up and dying.

Therapy is definitely something I need to look into when I get out of here. For Adrian.

He deserves a healthy mom. Maybe I can't give him a happy one, but I will do everything I can to be the best version of myself for him.

He deserves nothing less.

I'm just afraid that version is one that doesn't include being married to his dad.

Now that I know we're still married, I'm scared.

There was safety in knowing I didn't have to make the decision anymore.

Those fake divorce papers were my safety net.

Now it's gone and I'm left in limbo, completely helpless and terrified.

As if sensing the direction my thoughts are going, he enters the room, a sleeping Adrian on his chest. I look up, and for the first time in a week, I don't let my eyes fall away from his.

It's a subtle change but he catches it.

He's comes to a standstill, his hand still on the knob as he searches my eyes.

He must see something in them that has his jaw clenching and his blue eyes swimming.

In a flash, he sets our son in his crib and sits a few feet away from me on the edge of the bed, cautiously giving me the space I need to get through this conversation.

"Ree." He begins tentatively, voice hoarse with emotion.

My throat suddenly feels drier than the Sahara Desert and I have to shut my eyes to stop myself from breaking down. He's always been able to read my mind.

I may have loved that before, but now I loathe his ability to read me so easily.

My defenses are up, and I feel myself get angry once again.

In the back of my mind, I recognize the fact that my anger isn't fair to Noah.

He didn't do any of the things they said he did.

I don't want to lash out before we even have a conversation, but I can't seem to access that sensible part of my brain.

I don't even know if I have it in me to feel anything other than brainwashed. I'm in too deep, drowning in my trepidation and wallowing in my fears.

"Will you look at me? Please, Ree?" His whispered request cuts into me and my eyes fly open to find his face displaying so many emotions I get whiplash from it.

"Don't call me that."

I can't help it. When he calls me anything other than my name, the voice that urges me to kick him out of my room and my life starts screaming in my head.

It belies common sense. I don't get it either. This level of anger I have for him is consuming every part of me and we have yet to say more than a few words to each other.

"You're still my wife. I'm still your husband, Ria."

"On paper, Noah."

His shoulders set in a severe line and his gaze drops to my left hand.

"Where's your ring?"

"Where's yours?" I counter.

His hand goes to the collar of his shirt and he pulls out a chain with his wedding ring.

He's been wearing his wedding ring around his neck this whole time.

"Answer my question, Alessandria."

I raise an eyebrow, steeling him with a look. "I don't know. Ask Gabe."

He looks away and mutters a curse.

"Noah."

He looks back at me with such intensity in his eyes I have to swallow the meteoric lump lodged in my throat. I'm suddenly so damn thirsty.

I forget how handsome he is—how breathtaking it is to simply be in his presence.

He is so hot when he gets that determined glint in his eye.

I mentally shake myself against the conflict of emotions battling inside of me right now as

I do my best to school my face into a mask of indifference.

"Noah." I try again, with more conviction this time. "When are we getting out of here?"

"I'm working on it. Trust me."

I scoff, unable to stop myself from rolling my eyes.

Then the words come tumbling out.

"Trust, Noah? Trust who? Trust you? Are you seriously asking me that? I don't even know what the hell is going on." I lift my hands up in exasperation, unable to hold it in any longer. "I've been stuck here for over a year. This whole time thinking you put me here and trying to trust in that, in you, only to find out you had no clue I was even here. Your boss and best friend put me here without you knowing. All that training for what? All those months you would leave me for what? For them to easily kidnap me and force me in isolation? For what? And am I supposed to believe you suddenly finding me after all this time was coincidence? That you really had no idea I was pregnant or that you have a son?"

His eyes dance around me as my arms flail around, trying to get my points across.

All my repressed anger comes flooding out and I am powerless to stop it.

"And then you show up out of the blue, come in here and have the audacity to call me your wife? To stake some claim on me like we were never even apart? Do you have any idea what I've had to go through? Being alone. Pregnant and alone. A mother and alone. Not knowing when I would even be able to see past these walls? I don't even have a clue where I am--what state or city or even why I'm here in the first place. Anything and everything they've ever said to me alluded to you knowing what was best for me and for Adrian. So excuse me if I can't trust you, now or ever."

I shut my eyes, blowing out puffs of air, trying to calm the storm raging inside me.

I am so pissed.

For me. For Adrian.

For Noah but also at Noah.

At Gabe.

At the whole damn world.

Noah is silent but I feel him seething. He's not the only one who can read the other's mind.

We were together for five years, married for two of those. Three, if I count this last year we spent apart.

I can tell when he's angry, sad, hungry or horny.

And right now, he's pissed.

I let my eyelids flutter open.

He's staring at a sleeping Adrian. I see him swallow once, twice, three times.

His hands are gripping his knees, trembling with all the anger in the world.

His jaw tightens with determination as he turns back to me.

"Ria. I fucked up. I'm not going to make excuses for myself because you're right. I absolutely should have known that you wouldn't just leave me like that and that something happened to you. Instead, I let my fear of abandonment take over and believed in the idea they planted--that you left me and I wasn't enough. But I never stopped looking for you. I had every intention to beg for a chance to prove myself to you once I found you, so I kept searching."

He scoots closer to me on the bed until he's close enough to draw me into his arms, and he does. I'm stiff as a board but it doesn't deter him. He caresses my hair and back with his palms.

"I meant what I said to you, Ree--Ria. I will follow you to the ends of the earth because in case you forgot, you're it for me. Always have been, always will be. You and Adrian are everything to me." His arms tighten protectively until I'm cocooned in his warmth. "I am so sorry, baby. I know I have a lot to make up for. It was--is, my job to protect you. And I failed. I will not fail again. I promise you I will do everything to get you and Adrian out of here, safely. I want us to be a family. As soon as this case is done, I'm done with the bureau. I will find another job, something safe and secure. I will do anything and everything for you. Please believe in that. In me. I will wait for you, no matter how long it takes to forgive me."

I rest my forehead on his chest, pressing my palms into my eyelids to stop the tears from gushing out. But I lose myself in his embrace and once again, he rocks me against his chest. My arms snake around his waist of their own accord and I cling to him like a raft in a river. Willing myself to feel safe, I try to remember what that feels like.

He holds me for a while and I don't remember when but somehow, we end up on our backs. I'm bawling my eyes out, trying to find an outlet for all the emotions threatening to pull me under, and hoping that somehow this helps ebb the pain, fear, and anger.

But nothing happens.

The anger remains, and the fear increases.

The pain continues to have its hold on me, nearly suffocating me with its weight.

Noah

I pull the covers over a sleeping Ria.

My chest tightens, remembering her cutting words and the way she shook as she cried herself to sleep in my arms. I love this woman with everything I have.

I meant what I said to her. I'm finishing this job and then I'm done.

My job cost me her love, but it will not cost me her life or Adrian's.

As soon as we catch Sotnas and figure out who the mole is, I'm getting them out of here and doing everything I can to earn back her trust.

With one last lingering look at my sleeping wife and child, I grab the baby monitor and quietly leave the room.

I tip my head towards the bedroom where I pass Agent To, a signal for her to keep an eye and ear out. She has night duty and is setting up in the living room to start her shift.

It's merely a formality at this point, just an added measure to help Ria feel safe.

I've already swept the perimeter several times today and so has Gabe.

We alternate every two hours to ensure that nothing goes awry, considering we are operating with a much smaller team than normal.

A week ago, when I took over, I ran everyone's credentials.

Mina To and Ben Walker seemed like the safest options.

Upstanding records, both single, and both determined to move up the ranks of the agency.

And of course, clean financials.

Nothing that would allude to a payout by Sotnas for intel.

So I called my boss, who still owed me for what he did to me and to my family.

He didn't agree at first, livid that I was even in the know and that I was here.

It turns out Gabe couldn't handle the guilt and orchestrated Ria to have an "out" day so I would bump into her on my way back from another assignment.

To say he was in a lot of trouble would be an understatement.

But in the four years I've worked at the bureau, I've managed to make quite a few connections, including some very powerful ones. I've been incredibly lucky in my career. A year into being an agent, I was assigned as backup to a case involving a few senators who were being blackmailed after their personal computers were hacked. As a rookie agent, I was given the task of going through the paperwork to assist the lead agent on the case and that's when I stumbled on the link and was able to conclude who was behind the hack and blackmail. Since then, I've quickly gone up the ranks and even been awarded the FBI Medal of Valor by the Secretary of Defense. There was no way my boss could say no to my demands after I pulled the Secretary of Defense card.

My demands were simple: Four agents, including myself and Gabe.

At this point, betrayal or not, I needed someone I could trust with my family. He had kept them safe for this long, I'll give him credit there.

I also came up with a list of requests that Gabe was more than happy to fulfill.

Before the other agents were dismissed, they were given a list of things to buy separately as to not tip anyone who might be feeding the cartel information.

I spent a month undercover, trying to work my way into the cartel to get to Sotnas using whatever means I could, including bartering drugs and stolen goods. None of it proved to be lucrative. There was nothing substantial about the man himself-- not even his real name.

Sotnas was so elusive, I never even met him.

As far as I can tell, he had a revolving door of associates who did the dirty work for him.

He was never in the same place at the same time with any exchange that took place. He kept his hands clean of any actual selling and exchanging of illegal goods, which is why this whole thing is so suspicious.

Why target my wife when they could have gotten to me at any point during that month? And why would they want her alive but me dead?

If they were onto me then why didn't they take me out when they found me out? They certainly had every opportunity to do so.

Why target Ria when I was the one who was working the case? What good would that do?

Somehow, I feel like Ria is the key to this whole thing, which terrifies the fuck out of me.

What does Sotnas want with her?

I have yet to broach the subject with Gabe after we both spent the week trying to avoid another altercation. I still have the urge to kick his ass but I can acknowledge the fact that he kept my wife and son safe.

They're here and they're safe, away from anyone who would do them harm.

I intend to keep it that way.

I press my thumbprint into the pad just outside the basement door. I had Walker install it to keep track of the ins and outs of our base of operation.

And to prevent Ria from accidentally walking in and seeing anything.

I want to keep as much of this shit from her as possible.

My wife is a walking, breathing, ticking time bomb. Her fear is written all over her face.

It won't take much to push her over the edge of total panic.

It will take me years to undo what they did to her and I'm not about to add to it.

The green light just above the door handle indicates I'm permitted to open it and with one last nod to Mina, I walk in and shut the door behind me.

There are eight monitors propped on the wall on the left side of the room, where I head first. I scan and check every single one for signs of anything or anyone out of the ordinary.

"You did a periphery check?"

Gabe grunts behind me, his face buried under a pile of manila folders on the long table in the center of the room where he has set two years' worth of files on Sotnas and his cartel.

"Yeah, just got back five minutes ago."

"Walker?" I turn to Ben, who is behind another set of monitors on the other side of the room.

There are three in front of him. Ben Walker is the IT expert in our team while Mina To is our weapons expert.

Currently, he's running financial reports and checking all known data on the cartel, including their associates, to try and track anything that would indicate an opportunity for us to get to Sotnas himself.

He also goes over all the information being sent to us by our undercover agents who are keeping an eye out on the Cartel including surveillance footage on exchanges happening.

It's Ben's job to go through it every night and keep a log.

"Still the same pack and go. Same exchange but a different place and point of contact again."

Fuck. This guy is good.

How is he able to keep the rotation of associates doing his dirty work for him?

We still haven't figured that out.

The man doesn't even have a type.

One week it's a random teenager off the street and the next it's a single mom just trying to make some extra cash to feed her kids.

Nothing we can pin on him--no leads we can follow.

We have nothing conclusive to even further our investigation.

Sotnas and his cartel is currently the biggest distributor of illegal goods in the world. Name it and they barter it; drugs and stolen car parts being their primary products.

We managed to figure out that their distribution and manufacturing is mostly done in the US and that's when I was brought in undercover to try and infiltrate the cartel and get intel on the man in charge. Which was only time we had a break in the case when I stumbled upon a bigger exchange of stolen cars shipped from Asia on a barter.

After that, I was pulled out of the assignment so we could move in and make the arrest, but even then, the handful of his men we managed to bring in wouldn't sing.

Every single one of them is facing at least ten to twenty behind bars, each with a laundry list so long we couldn't make out a single charge that would connect to their boss or the cartel.

IN CASE YOU DIDN'T KNOW

Since then, it's been radio silence. He's been more careful, aside from the occasional drug sell.

Ben looks over his shoulder, motioning for me to come closer.

"There is one thing that stood out to me. Take a look at this."

Gabe gets up too and we both stand on either side of Agent Walker. Ben points at a series of photos of an older woman who looks to be in her fifties or sixties. She's carrying the type of tote bag you might get at a grocery store.

The photos show her walking and sitting on a bus bench.

Another series of photos show her looking around, and then setting the tote under the bench.

The same modus operandi as every other transaction but unlike the other drop-offs we've seen where the courier is quick to leave after, this woman remains seated.

This time, there are more than a dozen photos of this woman sitting on the bench beside the drop, looking around with her hands folded in her lap.

Our surveillance cameras are programmed to take photos every ten seconds so she must have stayed there for at least ten minutes.

This is odd. Something is off.

"Let's get to the set where she gets up and leaves."

Ben grins at me. "That's the thing. She doesn't."

Gabe straightens, quirking an eyebrow at me before looking back down at the monitor.

"Show us."

The next set of photos show the woman looking up and we catch the moment her mouth opens in surprise, like she says something out loud.

A burly man wearing a wool cap and a scowl can be seen in the next set. He has his shirt collar open to cover his face but his body language indicates he is not happy.

81

He sits on the other side of the bench, his leg touching the tote.

"Next," I spit out. I can feel the same burst of adrenaline I experience every time I get close to a break. I can practically feel this man's anger at this mistake in the transaction.

"Blow up the next set and zoom in on this guy."

Ben uses the mouse and zooms in.

My eyes search this next set of pictures and that's when I see it.

His sleeves are pulled up and a set of tattoos peek out.

Recognition dawns and I flash back to that first night with Ria.

"He's big and burly. A little bit taller than you, maybe six, five? He has blonde hair that's always in a greasy ponytail. Tattoos up and down his arms. One arm is covered in female cartoon characters. Like Betty Boop and Jessica Rabbit. And on the other is just a bunch of squiggly lines that I think are Celtic symbols? But he also has guns on that side... like a rifle with some sort of tag?"

CJ.

The guy who propositioned Ria and would have done worse, had I not been there with her.

Her roommate's slimy ex.

The link to figuring out what they want with Ria.

"I know him."

Two sets of eyes jump to me, and I shake my head in disbelief.

Coincidence?

I think not.

"What do you—" Ben gapes at me, his face showing signs of excitement and relief.

"Show me the rest. Then we'll talk about the sonofabitch."

Ben clicks through the next sets of photos, but nothing jumps out until the end. The bus hides them for a few sets until we have visual of them boarding the bus together. After the bus leaves, the tote is nowhere to be found, indicating a pickup was done.

I'm still shaking my head ten minutes later after I explain it to Ben and Gabe.

Ben is already on it. He's running everything he can find on CJ, tracking every place he's ever been.

Ben will find any digital print this guy has ever left online.

I stop right in front of our weapons wall, allowing myself to imagine pinning the asshole down and ramming his head with my gun.

There is no way he's just some random guy they picked to complete the transaction.

They slipped up, and something about that woman doesn't sit right either.

Something about the way CJ handled that whole thing was messy. Sloppy.

Ria.

I can't hide this from her. And if we're going to get this guy, I'm going to have to fill her in.

I'll have to bring her in here so she can tell us what she knows about this guy or even

see if she can ID any of the other runners or couriers.

I slam my hands down on the metal desk in frustration.

I hate this. Ria has been through enough.

But fuck, I can taste it. *This is it.*

The hole in their operation that we've been searching for years.

Ria is the key.

Gabe moves to stand on the other side of the table. He folds his arms, his stance determined and amped for a fight.

"Ria is the key to this whole thing."

With my head hung low, I glare at him.

This motherfucker knew.

"How long did you know he wanted her?"

Gabe's mouth presses in a grim line as he picks up a box from under the table and hands me the folder on the top.

I open it to find photos of Ria from over a year ago.

"What the fuck?" I growl.

I throw the folder on the table and grab another from the box and then another.

Halfway through the box, I stop.

Years worth of surveillance.

I try to draw air into my lungs.

They took photos of my wife for years.

There are even folders with photos of me from when I met Ria.

My head pops up to find Ben has stood up from his desk. His screen lights up as it searches for more information on CJ. He approaches us cautiously, probably wanting to be a buffer in case I lunged for Gabe's throat again.

"Where did you find this? And why do I not know about this?" I barely get the words out.

Ben and Gabe exchange looks before Gabe turns back to me with a resigned sigh.

"A few months ago, we followed a courier out to a harbor in Virginia. This was the first time a pickup happened close to where you lived. We figured it was worth a shot given the only time we had any progress with the investigation was when we found out he wanted to kidnap your wife and kill you. We lucked out. At that harbor was an abandoned furniture factory, and inside we found a production line of stolen car parts and a drug lab. We found all these files during the raid. One of the men we picked up admitted to it being one of Sotnas' spots, but that's all we could get out of him. He clammed up pretty quick and lawyered up."

I'm teetering on the edge of a freefall, frightened to my very core.

My wife—the love of my life.
He wants her.

Gabe releases a heaving breath.

"Noah. We thought he wanted her to get to you but it looks like he's been after her the whole time. The sight of those folders changed everything for me. They gave me clarity. We should—

I should have insisted we bring you here after they cleared your name. I fucked up. But I meant what I said, man. You and Ria are like family to me. There was no way in hell I was going to let him take her like that. I had every intention to bring you to Ria, but Director Villegas was determined to keep you off the case because of the ramifications. He assigned you case after case, so I just had to bide my time until there was an opening. I had to do it without him knowing I planned to lure you back here to your family."

Gabe shakes his head in disparagement at the folders.

"What the fuck does he want with her?"

A ping breaks through the silence in the room and Ben sits back at his desk to check it out.

"Well fuck."

I bristle. 'What-what is it?"

Ben twists in his seat to check the monitor that still has the transaction photos up.

He scrolls through the data, then sits back in shock.

"Colin Jester just crossed state lines from Missouri to Iowa."

That's close--too close to where we are.

"Where was he coming from?"

Somehow, I know what he's about to say next.

"The drop off that we just saw him do was in Ransom, Texas."

Gabe looks at me, his eyes widening at the realization.

Ransom was my last assignment before Gabe lured me here.

Sotnas is getting close, and that could only mean one thing.

Ria wasn't the only one being followed.

I was too.

~

LUCKILY, Gabe and I had enough training drilled into us that when I first came here, we made a few stops and circled around in the event we were being followed.

Regardless of how I felt at the time, my training was ingrained into me.

Safety and security come second nature to me.

Even if Sotnas did follow me to Nebraska, there was no way they could have followed us to the cabin without us noticing.

Walker and To also assured me that they weren't made on their way here with Ria and Adrian, but I wasn't going to gamble my family's lives based on assurances.

Within a few hours I secured backup. Again. But not before Ben ran a background check on them and I approved every single one assigned to support us on this case.

I have agents posted at the nearest town and in the clearing a few hundred yards away, along with a few who set up camp across the river from the cabin.

We've also clued in local enforcement.

CJ won't be able to enter the state without our knowledge.

Adrian stirs and my head clears instantly.

I gaze down at my son sleeping on my chest. He had slept through the night but woke up as I was entering the room, like he sensed his daddy in the room.

I bite my bottom lip hard enough to taste copper to keep the sobs from coming.

Now is not the time for me to break down and curse the powers that be for inflicting this on us.

I have to stay strong. I'm the one who's supposed to be in control and protect my family.

I shift Adrian to one arm, leaving the bottle I just used to feed him on the arm of the recliner.

I breathe him in, relishing in the sense of calm and surge of protectiveness I feel for this little guy. I set him down carefully in his crib, smiling at the gassy smirk he does in his sleep.

"Noah?"

I look up to find Ria sitting on the bed, the sheets tangled around her legs as she blinks at me with hazy eyes, fresh from a good night's sleep. I swallow the frown that threatens to show at the sight of the puffy purple bags under her eyes after having fallen asleep crying.

The shades in the room cast her in a glow that is almost as ethereal as that first morning we spent together, and my heart nearly leaps to my throat as my mind is filled with moments with her.

"Good morning beautiful," I murmur.

She rolls her eyes at me.

I almost laugh at that but then she stretches, one strap of her tank falling off her shoulder as the hem rides up, revealing an expanse of skin and giving me a peek at what I've been missing.

It's suddenly a hundred degrees in here and I clear my throat to soothe the unexpected dryness there.

Ria's arms fall to her side as she tilts her head and studies me.

An awareness fills the room, but she reads past my need for her, seeing right through me.

She straightens up, a deep frown marring her face.

"Did something happen?"

I offer her my hand, a sigh of relief passing through my lips when she takes it. Resting a knee on the bed, I pull her into my arms.

"Are you okay?"

Her breath tickles my neck and I allow myself to breathe in the familiar scent of her.

Roses and vanilla.

Fuck.

I missed this. Her. Us.

"I am now." I bury my nose in her hair, fulfilling my need to be just a little bit closer to her.

Fifteen months without her was torture.

Fifteen months without knowing if she was okay nearly drove me to madness.

But this is worse-- the uncertainty I feel at not knowing if I'm doing enough to keep them safe.

If I can keep them safe.

The tightness in my throat gets almost as unbearable as the beating my chest is being subjected to by the weight of my fear. I feel like my heart has been thrown into an incinerator.

It hurts to even fucking breathe.

"I love you so much, Ree."

She responds with a sharp intake of breath and a tremble.

Her hands trail up my chest and her right hand rests on my heart.

That's the only response I get from her. I squeeze her gently, letting her know it's okay.

I don't need her to say it back.

Even if my battered heart falls to my feet, I know it will take a hell of a long time to hear her say those words to me again.

But I know I will because damn it, we're meant to be.

And now the fear and uncertainty I felt just a few seconds ago are replaced with determination and resolve.

Nothing and nobody will ever take her from me again.

I will kill anyone who even dares try.

Ria

Something is wrong.

It's been a few days since I heard the crack in Noah's voice when he whispered that he loves me.

I've been waiting fifteen months to hear him say those words to me again.

But hearing them after everything that has happened had the same effect on me as a root canal.

Terrifying. Painful.

And that pisses me off because it shouldn't be this hard to love my husband again, especially after finding out he had no part in putting me here.

Something is up.

Noah refuses to let me or Adrian out of his sight. I'm sure he goes down to the basement when Adrian and I fall asleep at night but every morning when I wake up Noah's already in the room with us. Almost as if he never left.

And every morning when I wake up, Adrian is already changed, fed and bathed.

During the day, Noah is wherever we are.

If I'm in the bedroom with Adrian, he's on the recliner working.

If I'm in Adrian's playroom, he's there with us, on the floor playing with his son.

If we're in the living room, he's there.

It's like he can't stand to let us out of his sight. The circles under his eyes are getting darker and deeper, as though he hasn't slept, but he insists that he has.

Gabe and the other two agents have been holed up in the basement for the last few days, only surfacing to grab a bite or wash up.

And I swear when I looked out the living room window this morning, I recognized some of the people camping across from the cabin. It's like they've been here before, which means Noah recalled agents.

A chill runs down my spine.

I hate this--the distrust and fear of the unknown. I hate the feeling of being kept out of the loop again.

But it's tenfold now because I'm a mom and a wife.

I fear for the safety of my family as much as my own. Maybe even more.

I peek over my shoulder at Noah feeding Adrian in the living room. He insists we keep the drapes and blinds drawn, but he's definitely looking out the window like he's searching for something... or someone.

I need to get answers, but I know Noah won't give them to me willingly.

He won't outright lie to me either so there's only one way to get him to fess up.

A long-winded sigh comes out of me as I dump the vegetables in the pork sinigang I'm making for dinner.

Noah always loved it when I made Filipino dishes, like the first meal we had together. I'm trying in my own little way to show him that it may not be like it was but I still care.

And I'm hoping that through doing this, he gets that I'm trying and that he lets me in on whatever has everyone on edge, without being afraid of how I would react.

I WAS RIGHT.

Noah sneaks out at night.

I watch my husband tiptoe out of the room, leaving the door open just a sliver.

I'm not proud of it, but earlier I pretended I was falling asleep while he was rocking Adrian. I let him kiss me on the forehead afterward, wondering how many times he's done that in the last two weeks. I stayed as still as I could, slowing my breaths to an even pace to feign sleep as he lingered, his knuckles grazing my cheek.

I knew he was staring at me, watching me sleep, and I let him.

I grab the baby monitor, making sure the video camera is on and Adrian is visible. Then, I follow him out of the room. I'm greeted by Mina's surprised face as I pass her on the way out the door.

Clearly, she was getting ready to sit with us in the room as Noah's proxy, which just adds to my theory that something is wrong.

Especially when I spy her weapon on her hip.

"Ria, was there something you needed?" she asks quietly, stepping in front of me to block my way to the living room.

I quirk an eyebrow at her. We've gotten close these past few weeks and the slight pinch in between her eyebrows tells me she's stressed. Right now, she's on alert, which puts me on alert too. Knowing she would never forcefully keep me here, I nod my head towards the hallway, a silent way of asking her to let me through.

When she sighs in defeat, I give her a tight smile of gratitude.

"Please watch over Adrian. Excuse me."

I sidestep around her and head straight to the basement door.

I get there just as Noah is punching his fingerprint on the pad to unlock the door. I bypass him and open the door myself. I don't give him the chance to stop me as I run down the stairs, Noah's feet chasing behind me.

I stop at the bottom of the stairs, mindlessly scanning the room. I'm shocked at how quickly they put this room together when I could have sworn this basement was storage before.

I spin around to face Noah just as he's reaching for me. I take a step back, letting his hand fall.

A flash of something akin to hurt crosses his face, but he masks it with a faint smile.

I'm too caught up to focus on whether or not I just hurt his feelings because damn it, I deserve to know what's going on.

"Ria, what are you doing in here? I thought you were asleep."

"Forget that. Tell me what's got you so riled up, Noah."

Before he can answer me, something familiar on Agent Walker's monitor catches my eye. Ben notices me squinting my eyes, trying to get a better look, and he adjusts himself to cover the monitor.

For an FBI agent, he's not very slick.

Now *I know* they're hiding something from me.

Noah tries to block my path as I glare up at him.

How dare he keep more things from me?

"Ria, can we talk outside? Let the boys get back to work."

I shake my head in frustration and stomp over to Ben's desk.

Then I see *him*.

He looks exactly like he did six years ago, when he walked out of the condo I shared with his ex-girlfriend. Noah had driven him out, scaring the shit out of him.

I whirl around, gripping the desk for support as I look at Noah.

His eyes are shut, forehead creasing as he gulps in a huge breath.

"Noah. Wh-why-why is CJ on the monitor?"

I'm staring at my husband for what feels like forever when he finally opens his eyes to meet mine. "Do you want to sit down for this?"

His voice is laced with tension, face wracked with concern.

I shake my head again, unable to stop trembling all over.

"We have a theory, based on some evidence that came to light recently..."

Noah pauses, shoving a shaky hand through his hair and looking away.

I can feel the fear emanating from him, fear he's been trying to hide from me for days. He is no longer the composed man he was an hour ago, when he was holding our son.

Gabe takes the opening as Noah falls silent.

"We have reason to believe Sotnas is after you. That he was never after Noah. We think he was always after you."

I take a step back, hitting the desk behind me with a loud thump, and I have to grit my teeth to stop from crying out from the sting on my hip and the fear radiating through my body.

"Y-you think?"

This time, Ben speaks up.

"We know he's after you."

Ben shoves off his desk chair and offers his seat to me, but I can't move.

I'm paralyzed by all of this.

I feel a hand grasp my elbow as Gabe sits beside me, pulling the chair around for me to sit. I shake my head once, twice... a bunch of times, willing those last few words to go away. This can't be real. This can't be happening.

I don't even know *who* this Sotnas is.

Why me?

What does CJ have to do with this?

I'm a nobody—just a mom and wife who happens to be married to an FBI agent.

Gabe and the rest of the agents assured me repeatedly that the reason I was in witness protection was because I needed to be kept safe from the threats against my life brought on by Noah's undercover mission going south. For over a year, I repeated that in my head like a mantra, willing myself to trust in that. Until it became my life and now, they're telling me that this whole time, the bad guy's been after *me*?

That he's powerful enough for the FBI to have to protect me?

What about Noah?

Oh God. *What about Adrian?*

"Ria." It's a pained whisper. My husband looks as shaken up as I am.

He's falling apart before my very eyes.

He stands in front of me now, nodding at the seat.

I don't look away from him as I sit and continue to process. He gets down on one knee in front of me, looking down at my hands curled around the baby monitor. He lays one hand on them to stop them from shaking and the other pulls the monitor from my grasp.

"Noah... what-why is he after me? And what does CJ have to do with it?"

He shakes his head and swallows hard, as he stares at our son sleeping on the monitor.

"We're still working on the why. We haven't figured that out yet but-"

"Then how do you know he's after me?"

Noah's jaw tightens, his shoulders growing more tense.

He shakes and stutters as he tries to come up with the right words.

After a long pause, he stills, taking a deep, shuddering breath and collecting himself.

He sets the monitor on the desk next to me and gets up, holding out his hand for me to take. And I do. He takes me to the metal desk in the middle of the room, filled with folders and marked boxes.

The other men are quiet as they watch us, so silent and intense that you could cut the tension with a knife and hear it slice, the sound bouncing off the walls.

Noah pulls out a box from underneath the table and wordlessly asks me to look into it.

I pick up the first folder from the stack in the box and open it.

My eyes widen as my stomach turns sour.

The fear eats at me, clawing from the inside until I can practically feel it crawling on my skin.

I continue my search as I open another folder, and another, until I've reached the end of the box.

The box contains almost the entirety of my life.

He's been watching me this whole time. *Why?* Who is he?

I'm breathing so hard and so loud I'm afraid I'll pass out from the sheer force.

Noah's fingers gently ease mine off the last folder as he grabs the stack and places them back inside the box. He leads me back to the desk, moving the chair to the side so it's facing half of the room and the desk.

He sits me down again, easing back onto his knee.

"Who is he, Noah?"

"The illusive leader of the Sotnas cartel. He owns the majority of illegal trade stateside, exporting and importing in at least three continents."

"But who is he?"

"We still don't know. He eluded us for years. He's smart in how he operates, handling everything through associates and picking randoms to do his dirty work for him. We don't even have a name or a face to go on."

Gabe leans on the metal desk, crossing his arms.

"The only breaks we've ever had on this case are all linked to you, Ria. That text, this box and now this guy, who Noah says you know."

I rub my palm across my forehead, trying to follow this conversation. I am so confused and terrified.

"What is CJ's part in all of this?" I bite the inside of my lip to keep it from trembling as I attempt to keep my focus on this horrifying conversation.

Ben speaks up from his perch on the wall with their weapons.

"We've been monitoring the drops the Sotnas cartel has been doing for the last two years. That's how we found the box containing evidence that he's been watching you. We have been careful not to move in because we don't want to risk tipping him off. But the last transaction was done so close to where you and Noah lived, we decided the coincidence was enough to get a warrant."

"Yet another link to you," Gabe offers quietly.

"I still don't get--"

I feel Noah squeeze my hand and I turn to look back at him. His eyes are observing me tentatively, like he's searching for the right words. I watch as his shoulders set in determination and his eyes glint with such intense force I have to blink twice.

"Last week, a drop occurred but the regular MO, which is usually a drop and go, was not followed. They broke protocol. The interaction between the runner and courier was odd enough for Ben to flag it in the system. As soon as he showed me the photos, I recognized him. I'd never forget a face, Ria--

especially one who threatened your safety. The tattoos helped identify him."

"Show me."

Noah starts to shake his head like he doesn't want to overwhelm me. I ignore him and turn to Ben, who is watching our exchange with hesitation.

"Show me." It's a command, not a request.

After a beat, Ben moves to stand next to me as he scrolls through one of the monitors.

Then he pulls up a series of photographs that have me squinting at the monitors yet again.

Then my heart drops to my feet.

I gasp as a shiver runs down my spine.

"I–I know her."

"Wait, what?" This comes from Gabe, who suddenly materializes next to Ben.

"Aunt Patty."

I look over at Noah, whose eyes are as wide as mine, trepidation written all over his face. He knows exactly who I'm talking about.

He never met her, because once she shipped my stuff off to Virginia, she washed her hands of me. She didn't even bother responding to calls or texts, or even our wedding invitation.

But Noah knows of her. I've talked about her enough for him to get the significance.

"Who is she?"

Gabe gawks at me, his eyes flying back and forth between me and Noah.

I nod, swallowing the lump that has formed in my throat.

"She was my mom's best friend. I lived in her condo during college, after my mom died.. The guy? CJ? He was her daughter's ex-boyfriend."

Ben clears his throat and we all look at him in unison.

"I hate to be the one to point this out, Noah, but we need Ria in here."

Noah curses under his breath, his jaw locked as he gives Ben a terse nod.

"Compile all the photos we have of every transaction within the last year and a half. Up until right before I got assigned this case. Include any records we have of deals made near all Ria's addresses. Also, run a check on Patty up to the last two decades. Let's cover the time she became close with Ria's mom. Aside from the obvious, let's form a connection here. We need to find out what this bastard wants with Ria, and why it's surfacing now."

Noah turns to look at me, his eyes sad and resigned.

"We need to know everything you know about Patty and CJ."

My eyes start to sting with unshed tears as a thought occurs to me.

"What about Penny? She must be a connection too?"

"On it. Just write down anything you remember. Dates. Names. Nicknames. Addresses. Work. Anything helps." Ben interjects, "I'll run every known associate, family member, and partner to find a commonality."

Ben taps me on the shoulder as Noah wraps an arm around me. He helps me up and Ben takes over the vacant seat.

Ben starts tapping on his keyboard as boxes start showing up on all three monitors, indicating he's running multiple searches through their system.

Gabe hands me a pen and paper.

I write down what I know about them, which isn't much.

"Ria?" Noah props his hands on the desk beside me, leaning close and whispering. "Can you write down information about your mom too? I think we need to determine that connection too."

I nod, swallowing through the tears that are now running down my cheeks.

Noah is breathing hard, his hands gripping the desk, and I know he's doing everything he can to stop from grabbing me and taking me out of this room.

Ben looks over his shoulder as Gabe hands him the notes I just finished writing.

"Get some sleep, Ria. You too, Noah. It's going to take a few hours. We'll go through all of this in the morning. Gabe can help me out here."

Noah nods at Gabe as he grabs the baby monitor, holding his hand out for me to take.

"Thank you," I whisper to the men who are helping keep me and my family safe.

I'm grateful for them, but also terrified of what they might find.

They both give me nods. Ben goes back to his computer as Gabe goes through the files on the desk.

As soon as Noah gets me out of the basement and into the living room, he stops. His arm comes around my legs as he lifts me. He holds me close to his chest as sob after sob wracks through me.

Before I know it, we're back in our room. Caught up in the whirlwind of my emotions, I miss the part where Mina leaves the room. Noah lays me down on the bed gently, kissing the top of my head.

"Let me check on the little guy real quick. Lay down, baby."

I shut my eyes, unable to grasp reality.

I've lived my whole life in fear, and now my life is *actually* in danger. And not just as a byproduct of Noah's job.

I cover my face with both of my hands as I curl up into a ball, unable to keep the tears from flowing. They're hot on my skin and salty on my open mouth as I try my best to keep from screaming out loud.

My son. My poor son. What's going to happen to him?
Does Sotnas know about him? Does he want him too?
Does he still want to kill Noah to get to me? Will he?
Adrian. I can't lose him. I can't.

I will do anything to keep my son safe and away from this horrible man who has stalked me.

Strong arms come around me and before I can blink, Noah has turned me in his arms. He's sitting with his back on the pillows, holding me and rocking me in his lap. One of his hands goes through the strands of my hair while the other rubs my back. I try to focus on the sensations they evoke, but a single thought keeps me in this limbo of fear.

My husband has always been overprotective of me, a result of only having each other for years.

But now, we have Adrian to consider.

"N-n-noah?"

He hums, but I can feel his chest beating fast and hard under my cheek.

I place a trembling hand on it. "Promise me something?"

I manage to calm down enough to get the words out.

He stiffens like he knows what's coming, and he probably does.

In the years we were together, we always somehow knew when one of us needed something. We rarely fought, and when we did, one of us always caved, unable to stand the silence and tension between us for more than an hour or two. When he left on assignment, we were in a good place, which made living apart for over a year truly unfathomable.

"Promise you what, baby?" He echoes my whisper.

"That whatever happens, you'll protect Adrian."

"Ree...," he croaks.

"I mean it, Noah. If it comes to it, leave me. Take Adrian and run."

"I can't do that, Ria. I need you. Like I fucking need oxygen to survive. You're what anchors me. Keeps me steady. Sane. You keep me going, even when the tides are against me. I would drown without you."

My eyes shut from the impact of his words, but I need to stand my ground here. I need to strengthen my resolve because this is Adrian's life we're talking about here.

I open my eyes to find him shaking his head, his eyes boring into mine, begging me to reconsider.

I can't.

I draw back from his arms and kneel on the bed next to him.

"Promise me, Noah."

My eyes are transfixed on his. He's staring back at me, bewildered and distraught, tears now running down his cheeks.

"Ria. Please, please, don't make me abandon you again."

I straighten my back, my knuckles digging into the sheets as I continue to stare at him.

My gaze is clear now. My mind is made up.

"It wasn't your fault. What happened was not your fault-- I get that now. In fact, now that we know this is because a mad man is after me, it's actually my fault. Adrian cannot-- will not—be collateral damage. You need to protect him. He's your son."

"And you're my wife," he grits out. He straightens too.

Anger and frustration mar his features, but it doesn't deter me.

"Adrian comes first, Noah."

"Again, you are my wife, Ria. You think it's easy for me to walk away and leave you?"

He leans in, gripping my chin with a callused hand. "In case you didn't know, you are my life."

He spits out each word, his eyes boring into mine.

His other hand wraps around my cheek, fingers gripping the back of my head tightly.

"And in case you forgot, or need a reminder, nothing has changed for me. I will not promise anything that takes you away from me again. You. Me. Adrian. That's it. All or nothing."

"All or nothing?" I choke out. "We cannot gamble our son's life like that, Noah. Please."

He shakes his head at me, his eyes wild, looking everywhere but at me. He practically vibrates with repressed anger.

Then he pauses as he stares at our sleeping son.

I follow his gaze and almost choke on the onslaught of tears. A tsunami of emotions have me shutting my eyes, my lips pursed as I clutch my stomach to try and stop the pain and fear from drowning me.

"Please, Noah. If you truly love me, you will do this for me."

A shuddering, low growl comes out of Noah. "And if you loved me, you wouldn't ask me to live my life without you again or make our son live a life without his mother."

My eyes are still shut tight, but I feel him leave the bed, and then leave the room.

He left me.

Again.

Noah

I didn't mean to walk out on her, but I wasn't about to stay and listen to her tell me she's willing to sacrifice herself, her life and being with us to keep Adrian safe.

She's my wife, damn it. My life. Mine.

I already lived a nightmare of a year without her. I can't do it again.

I *need* her. *Adrian* needs her.

I want to scream and punch something, but I can't.

Deep down, I know she's coming from a place of love and her inherent need to be selfless. She puts others first. It's one of the reasons I fell for her.

Memories of our life together flood my mind as I almost cry out, not willing to think our best years are behind us and now all we have are memories.

I continue to pace the living room, my fingers practically clawing through my hair as I attempt to get a grip. My feet feel like lead, my footsteps heavy with the weight of it all. I'm wearing a hole on the carpet, probably making it sound like a stampede in the basement.

I stand by the window, pulling the curtain back to check on our backup.

The three fire pits signaling it's safe are all still burning. If a breach happens, the fires would go out, letting us know to be on guard.

IN CASE YOU DIDN'T KNOW

Warmth floods me and I feel her presence before I hear her.

"Noah."

I scrub a tired hand across my face, surprised when I realize it's wet. I didn't realize I had been crying, caught up in my wife's outrageous demands.

"Noah." Ria's voice is louder now, commanding. "Look at me."

I slowly turn to look at her, folding my hands into fists to keep from reaching for her. I want nothing more than to gently shake some sense into her, but the last thing I want to do is lash out or hurt her.

"You can't just leave like that. Haven't you learned anything?"

I square my shoulders back, my pathetic hold on my emotions breaking.

"You want to know what I learned?" I cross the room to her, looming over her, purposely using my height to prove to her that I am more than capable of protecting her. "My life is absolute shit without you. Now that I've found you and Adrian, nothing and no one will ever keep us apart again. I won't allow it. It's you and me, baby. None of the time we spent apart has changed that. Until the ends of the earth, Ria. I'll always be there to catch you."

I take a step back after using the same words I told her years ago, hoping it gets through to her beautiful stubborn head.

Ria's eyes widen with awareness and she takes me in.

Her gaze rakes over me, sweeping past my clenched fists and rigid shoulders and pausing on my mouth. Then her eyes fly back to mine, and I see my every emotion I feel mirrored back to me.

Anger.

Fear.

Disappointment.

Lust.

I don't think about it. My body moves on its own. Her's must too because she meets me halfway.

We both groan as our lips meet in a dance, starting out slow but quickly turning combustible.

Finally.

I grip the back of her head and her arms curl around my neck as our mouths nip and tug.

I swoop down to lift her as my free arm wraps around her waist and her legs go around mine.

I back her into the wall, not breaking the kiss.

This kiss took fifteen months to happen, but it feels like every other one we've shared. It's like no time has even passed between us.

We still connect like I've never connected with anyone else.

She still tastes like everything and feels like everything.

The fires we stoke in one another are burning hot and wild.

My lips trail down her neck and she arches her back, driving me absolutely wild.

I feel her hands run down my chest as she fists my shirt.

Then I remember the cameras.

I lean my forehead on hers, regaining control.

"Baby, unless we want to give the other agents a show, I suggest we go to the bedroom."

She doesn't say anything, but I can feel her drawing staggering breaths. I lean back enough to see that her eyes are wide. Her hands flatten on my chest as she gives me a little push and her legs untangle themselves around my waist.

I set her back down on the floor and when she simply stares at her feet, I am hit with the realization that she is regretting this. I take a step back, shoving my hands in my gray sweats and ignoring the telltale signs of my own arousal to give her space.

Finally, after seconds that feel like hours that feel like weeks, she nods her head and turns towards the room.

I'm stuck, not knowing if I should follow or wait until I cool down, when she looks over her shoulder. She tips her head, and her eyebrows meet.

"Are you coming?"

I give her a terse nod and quietly follow her. With the way I feel right now, it's like I'm standing over the precipice and it wouldn't take me long to free-fall right off it.

I shut the door behind us and as she makes for the bed, I head straight to the recliner.

Mentally preparing myself for another sleepless night, I lower myself down on a space I've called my bed for weeks. I don't dare ask Ria for a spot on the bed for three reasons.

First, I don't want to push her. The fact that she even thought of divorcing me means I have a lot to make up for when it comes to winning her back. Ria has the softest and kindest heart I've ever known. If I ask to sleep beside her, she will let me, regardless of how she feels. *That* would not be fair to her. She's still hurting, regardless of my part in it, I still did it. It's still a reality she lived with.

Second, the temptation of her being mere inches away would be too much for me. Just being around her is hard enough.

And third, shutting my eyes would be too much of a risk. I need to be awake to watch over my family and make sure nothing happens to them. I can't do that while asleep.

"You're exhausted."

My eyes fly up and find Ria standing right in front of me with an outstretched hand.

Did I doze off? Did I say that out loud?

With her probing eyes, I realize she's reading me as easily

as she always has, picking apart my brain before I even have a chance to pinpoint what I'm feeling.

I stare at her, letting myself drink in the sight of her. I allow myself to finally get a good look at the woman who stole my heart years ago and never returned it.

Ria's eyes are still the prettiest I've ever seen, soft brown eyes that burn with so much emotion, I lose myself in it. Her hair is longer now. Her hourglass figure is gone, her frame much thinner.

I've been afraid to ask, but I want to know about the last fifteen months of her life.

I want to know every moment she cried, every single second of fear she had.

All the moments that were stolen from us—good and bad.

I want to know every pregnancy craving she had and how Adrian's birth was. I want to know when he first lifted his head, first laughed, first sat on his own and just… everything.

Ria clucks her tongue at me, disapproving of my lack of response. She reaches over and grabs my hand, tugging me towards the bed.

When we get there, she lets go and remains standing, her brows meeting in concern and frustration.

"On the bed, Noah."

I'm still staring at her as I perch on the edge of the bed, confused.

"Ree?"

With a heavy sigh, her hands go to her hips and her eyes flitter around my face.

"Noah. You've clearly not slept in days. Your body is exhausted. Your mind is overworked."

She gives me a gentle shove.

"Lay down."

The tone of her voice brooks no judgment, but the double meaning in her words makes heat coil low in my belly. My face must belie my thoughts when one of her eyebrows quirks up.

"I'm not ready, Noah." She whispers hesitantly, her eyes shining.

I take her hand in mine, gently rubbing the pad of my thumb on her knuckles.

"It's okay, baby. I understand—"

"No, you don't Noah," she interjects, pulling her hand back. "I don't-I don't know if I will ever be ready to be intimate with you... or anyone like that ever again."

I try to ignore the sting of her words, especially after she added *anyone* to that sentence. The thought of her not feeling safe with me is already unbearable, but the thought of her even thinking of being with anyone else is downright excruciating.

There's really nothing I can do or say at this moment to assure her we will get back to *us* again. I lie down and stare at the ceiling trying to bury the pain and longing away but it still ebbs and flows inside me.

I hear a choking sob and before I realize the sound is coming from me, she crawls into my arms. She buries her face in my neck and her arms wrap around me until we're both clinging to each other. Her breath fans my neck as I feel her hot tears dampen my shirt.

"I'm sorry, Noah. I shouldn't-shouldn't have said anyone. I just mean—I'm not there yet and I'm worried. I don't know if I can ever get there."

Her hands frame my face, and she gazes into my eyes for a long time before she speaks again.

"I know this is just as hard and terrifying for you as it is for me. I know you. I know the weight of protecting us is keeping you awake, but that's exactly why you need to rest. Because we need you. We need you alert and at a hundred percent in order to get us out and through this. This—this whole thing is way beyond my wildest nightmares but never for a single second do I doubt your ability to keep us safe. I just—I'm scared, Noah, and the only way I can feel even a tiny smidge of release from fear is if you promise me that no matter what happens, our son comes first. That you will protect him first."

This woman holds my heart. I'm powerless to do anything but follow her lead.

I nod, even though my heart breaks at the mere thought of being without her again.

She gives me a small, teary smile. "Whatever happens, just think about the fact that our love made something as beautiful—" she glances over her shoulder at Adrian, "—as our son."

I choke out another sob as I pull her against me, my nose pressed to her hair, trying to center myself with her scent and the feel of her skin against mine.

"Thank you, Noah."

With that she hands me back my heart and it shatters in the space between us.

Ria

He's hurting.
His heart is breaking.
I did that.

I hastily swipe at the errant tears running down my face as I watch Noah sleep beside me.

He fell asleep holding me, the tears drying on his face as he succumbed to his exhaustion.

I know what he wants from me, and even though I desperately want to meet him halfway, my fear is overtaking everything.

I had always been afraid of intimacy. Forming connections and building relationships isn't something I was ever good at. Anytime someone got close enough, I always felt like I was hanging on the edge of the cliff and they were on the other side daring me to jump. In the end, I always walked away because the possibility of getting hurt was too great for me to risk.

I grew up with a mom whose whole world revolved around me so when she died, I surrendered to that fear.

Until Noah came and I felt safe enough in his ability to catch me.

I need to know that he and Adrian are safe. I have no idea what this Sotnas wants but it can't be good. That's not a risk I'm willing to take. He already threatened Noah's life once. If

I have to bargain myself in the process, that's what I'm prepared to do. I would sacrifice myself over and over again for my family.

The fact of the matter is, Noah saved my life then gave me one worth living.

∼

MORNING COMES QUICKLY, and before I know it, I'm back in the basement with all four agents . Gabe is going over the surveillance cameras, cross-checking the footage with something on the huge tablet on his arm. Mina is hunched over the corner desk, cleaning weapons and making eyes with Ben, who is pretending not to notice. His eyes are glued to his monitors. But every now and then, he steals a look over his shoulder, his gaze zeroed in on her.

My eyes trail beside him to my husband. Noah brought the playpen in here and I watch as he sets Adrian down for his afternoon nap.

This morning, for the first time in weeks, I woke up before him and he was still passed out beside me when I got up to feed and change Adrian.

He obviously needed the rest.

Noah straightens, looking over his shoulder at me. He tries to give me a reassuring smile that comes off like a grimace, and I know he's remembering our conversation last night. His reluctance to get me involved is plastered all over his face.

But I very much am involved. I am, begrudgingly, the subject of this whole case and the

only leverage the FBI has.

Noah looks down at me, reaching out to squeeze my hands gently.

"I'm right here, okay? If it gets to be too much, just let me know."

I blow out a breath. "I'm ready."

GABE LETS the last box of files fall down to the floor with a thump. He curses under his breath as he kicks the box under the desk.

"So, nothing?"

"I'm sorry. Maybe I can go through it again?"

"We've gone through it three times now, Ria. If you don't recognize any of them by now, chances are you don't know any of them."

I nod, feeling completely useless. How do I not have the slightest clue why this man is after me? Am I that clueless?

I look over at Noah and find him deep in thought as he paces next to Adrian's crib. He has a thoughtful expression on his face, like he's trying to figure something out.

After a few more minutes of absolute silence, I open my mouth to say something when Noah whirls around and grabs the box containing the surveillance photos Sotnas had taken of me.

He takes out half of the folders and then starts rummaging through the rest of the box. I hesitantly take a step towards him but Gabe gently tugs my elbow back and shakes his head at me.

"Let him be. This is his process. He knows what he's doing," Gabe whispers in my ear.

I have never seen Noah in his element.

He's intense. Laser focused.

Almost *feral*.

His jaw is ticking, mouth pursed in thought and when he seemingly finds what he's looking for, he strides across the room to Ben.

Ben is still running information I gave him last night. He's trying to piece together two decades worth of information between my mom, Aunt Patty and Penelope.

"Here. Find me what you can about this woman, right here. See if you can draw a match to a courier."

Gabe had labeled the folders by month and year.

Noah pulled out all the folders of the year we met.

I don't remember the day, but Noah does. He pulled pictures of me helping a mother out with her groceries in the parking lot of the café I used to work at. Then he had Ben cross reference it with surveillance photos and came up with a match.

A random person I helped was a courier?

"Noah?"

His mouth is set in a grim line as he settles his palms on the metal desk between us.

"I need you to try not to panic, okay?"

I nod, my gaze flitting between him and Adrian, who's in his playpen playing and watching a TV show on a tablet.

"I need you to write down every single person you remember coming across. Every landlord. Every boss. Every coworker or friend you've ever had."

Mina hands me a pen and paper.

I stare at it for a bit. My hand is shaking so much, I can't write a single letter.

I feel Noah move to stand behind me. His arms snake around my waist while he buries his face in the crook of my neck.

I don't remember everyone, especially last names of people I worked with, but the ones I do remember are landlords and bosses. I stopped having friends in high school after Mom got sick, and I ended up having to stay home or work to take care of her.

My list of acquaintances is close to nothing.

I do my best to write what I do remember with a less than steady hand. As soon as I'm done, Noah takes the paper from my hand and adds a name to it.

I recognize the name as the real estate agent who sold us our house.

Ben takes the list and adds it to his search, more windows populating his screens.

A series of pings slash through the room. Ben straightens in his seat, his eyes zeroed in on the information generating on the middle screen. His fingers fly across his keyboard and he starts moving windows to the left screen as he gestures for Gabe to approach his desk.

I'm about to ask what's going on when Noah's fingers thread through mine as he grips my hand in his. He raises it to his lips, gently kissing my knuckles.

I don't know if it's the sensation of his touch on my skin, but for a moment I feel peace. I stare at my husband's eyes as he stares into mine and the rest of the world stands still.

Everything around us ceases to exist.

My gentle giant. I fell for this man hard and fast.

Even with the chaos of the last year, I know I will never love someone as much as I love him. There are too many things left unsaid between us—too many variables that keep us apart.

Yet he remains steady, vulnerable, and mine.

Without a second thought, I step into him. His other hand automatically comes around to wrap me in his embrace, his thumb caressing the small of my back in soothing circles.

We continue to stare at each other for a good while.

My chin resting on his chest. My hand still in his.

For a moment, we lose ourselves in the peace we find only in each other.

I know in the back of my mind our lives will be punctured once again with whatever Ben has found out, so I allow myself this moment to simply look at Noah.

I try to convey what my heart desperately wants to tell him, despite my brain urging me to fight against it. The small smile he gives me tells me he knows. He gets it.

He understands my needs even if they're completely opposite of his.

"Noah."

Noah's head swivels at Ben's urgent tone, but his gaze holds mine for a fraction of a second before he squeezes me and lets me go to stride across the room to his colleagues.

Needing a breather before hearing bad news, I turn around to check on my son.

Noah

I ease my hold on Ria, reluctantly letting her go.

I can tell by the urgency in Ben's tone that whatever information he dug up can't be good.

Gabe moves to stand by the wall adjacent to Ben's desk, grabbing all the new evidence spewing out of our printers. Out of the corner of my eye, I see Mina crossing the room to join us.

The printers beep, signaling the end of the printing cycle and when I make to check the papers, Ben freezes, hastily pointing at something on his screen that makes my skin crawl.

My heart drops to my feet. Tearing my gaze away, I look over at Gabe. He looks away from the monitors, his eyes wide as he shakes his head at me, resignation written all over his face.

"Ria." My voice comes out hoarse and I clear my throat.

My wife stiffens as she covers a now sleeping Adrian with a tiny blanket. Clutching the side of the playpen, her eyes meet mine slowly and what she sees has her trembling.

I tip my head at Gabe, motioning for him to clear the metal desk so we can huddle there.

I nod my head at Mina, pointing to the surveillance wall and she immediately grabs the tablet.

I grab two of our burner phones, tossing one to Ben and

the other to Gabe. They know what to do. Without waiting for confirmation, I cross the room to Ria. I gently tug her down to sit on the chair next to Adrian's playpen. Once again, I kneel in front of her and quietly search her eyes.

"Noah?" She utters my name in a shaky whisper.

"CJ has been spotted in Des Moines, Iowa. In a private airfield."

I pull Ria's hands tight against my chest.

"And he's not alone."

~

GABE chucks the burners into the bin marked 'used'. For obvious reasons, we don't use the phones more than once before we discard them. Ben gets up from his desk to grab the tablet from Mina, who is reentering the basement from the clearing outside after informing our backup of the situation. They all huddle and go over all the new evidence we have.

I know I need to be there with them but I have my hands full at the moment.

I'm cradling my wife on my lap. I barely got the words out about CJ before Ria collapsed and started hyperventilating. Thankfully, Adrian stayed asleep throughout all this.

Fuck.

I have a plan, but I know Ria will fight me on it. I'm not keen on it either but it's the best course of action. Gabe and I have already gone through all the variables, and collectively, the four of us decided this would ensure Adrian's safety.

So yeah... *fuck.*

We need to be ready. And fast.

We're running out of time.

Ria's grip on my shirt loosens as her breaths slow down.

She leans away from me, dabbing her wet cheeks with the sleeve of her shirt.

I give her a lingering kiss on the temple before pulling her up and leading her over to the table.

Ben has organized everything he found out about her mom and her Aunt Patty's relationship, including their lives before and after they met.

I set my hands on the desk. "Alright. Talk to me. What do we have? Everything good?"

Mina speaks up first in her usual, no-nonsense tone. "All clear. The campsite is preparing for a possible ambush, as we speak. I have three agents posted upstairs right now, and the rest are outside securing the perimeter."

Mina nods at Ben, who is leaning on the wall by the printers, to continue.

"I've spoken with local enforcement and sent them photos we have of every individual at the airstrip. They are prepared to back us up and flag any suspicious arrivals. I've also informed the state. Same thing. If and when they cross state lines, we'll be the first to know.. The system is still running visuals but we have enough to get a warrant to arrest CJ should they cross paths with him."

"Perfect. Can you print those photos from the airfield? Let's see if anyone matches with what we have here or if Ria recognizes any of them."

Ben nods and quickly makes his way to his desk.

I turn to Gabe, who has his jaw locked, tension radiating from every inch of him. I quirk an eyebrow in question. I'm not sure what has him so annoyed.

"Director Villegas is aware. He's securing you a different location to move to if the need arises."

That fucker. I knew the director would try to pull Gabe.

But Gabe and I have an understanding. He's staying with us until the end.

"Alright. Well, that's more than I expected from him."

Bending my elbows, I lean close to my wife and whisper, "Let's go through these. There must be something here that can help us."

I squeeze Ria's hand gently, once again hit by how small and fragile she is.

"Are you ready, or do you need more time?"

She shakes her head, not even bothering to look at me as she lets go of my hand to stand next to Ben, who has returned to the table with a stack of photos.

She sifts through everything slowly and methodically when all of a sudden, she pauses. She lets out a sharp gasp. A crease starts to form on her forehead as her back stiffens. Her movements become more frantic as she starts stacking papers one on top of the other.

I'm tempted to break her trance, but I can practically see her placing the final piece of the puzzle.

"Wha-what's the cartel's name again?"

"Sotnas," Mina supplies with a perplexed look.

Ria shuts her eyes, her chin trembling as a lone tear falls down her cheek.

"Noah... what's my full name?"

"Alessandria Santos Halliwell Thomas."

My wife's eyes flutter open and her gaze locks with mine.

"What's my middle name?"

A chill tickles down my spine and I feel uneasy.

"Santos?"

She's trying to tell me something but it's not connecting. Something lurks behind her eyes and the only thing I can focus on is the horror in them. It has me slowly dying inside as the last remnant of hope in me withers. The earlier rush of adrenaline I felt at her possibly figuring something out comes crashing down.

Gabe slams a clenched fist on the table. "Fuck! How did we miss this?!"

Apparently, he's quicker than I am.

Anger takes over, and if not for my son sleeping, I may have turned this table already and lunged for the photos.

"Will someone please tell me what the hell is going on?"

The table tempts me.

Ria starts to shake, wrapping an arm around herself and handing two photos to Ben.

Ben's eyes widen and he hands them to me.

The first one is a picture of Ria's mom--I recognize her because Ria is the spitting image of her--but a much younger version, possibly in her early twenties. She's with a man around the same age inside a posh restaurant. They look cozy and happy as they smile for the camera.

The other photo is from the airstrip. In the photo, CJ is talking to a man who looks to be in his fifties, surrounded by armed bodyguards.

The man CJ is talking to is the same man in the photo with Ria's mom.

"Noah."

I don't look up. I can't.

I'm horrified. Frightened.

Ria is in deeper than we even knew.

This man will not stop until he gets her.

I throw the photos on the desk, tucking my wife in my chest.

She never knew her father but she's aware that her middle name is his.

And she knows what he looks like based on a photo her mom kept.

A single photo. *That* photo.

The very same one I had come across on our first night together. The one on her bedside table.

Then it clicks.

Sotnas read backwards is *Santos.*

Ria's father.

He's been watching her this whole time because Ria is his daughter. And now for some reason, he's decided he wants her back.

He will stop at nothing.

He's taking back what was stolen from him.

∼

We spent the next three hours going through every piece of evidence we have.

After the first hour, we still had no concrete link until Ria noticed something.

Once again, none of us pieced it together until somehow, she did.

At first, she pointed out little things like more than a few of the runners had the same tote bag from an independent grocery store across the street from her café.

Then, she noticed some of the younger couriers were wearing her college's school colors.

She asked us to check if any of the couriers or runners lived in the area at one point in their lives.

Turns out, every single one, even the ones who were doing drop offs and pick-ups outside the state had, at some point, lived in her neighborhood.

When we got to the information we had on her Mom, Ria shut down.

She may still have been there physically, but emotionally, she became a wall.

Mina helped her go through everything including what we found out about her Aunt Patty.

It turns out that her mom had met Patty a few months

after she had Ria, at the same restaurant she had previously dined in with Santos.

After Ben determined an accurate timeline based on our evidence, we figured out Ria's mom had lied about how she met Santos. The first time they met was in Washington State, not the Philippines. She went with him to the Philippines later, where it looked like they had a falling out.

No records show them meeting up again.

A year later, she befriended Patty.

If I was hazarding a guess, Patty was hired by Santos to keep an eye on his former lover and child.

I rub the back of my neck as I watch Ria busy herself in the kitchen. She cooks when she's stressed.

After a few hours, Adrian started getting fussy and Gabe ordered us out of the basement.

Rolling my shoulders back, I approach her from behind as she stirs the wok.

I slowly wrap an arm around her waist, bending my knees to account for our height difference. I rest my chin on her shoulder.

Landing a gentle kiss on her cheek, I once again lay it all out for her.

"Please trust me? Trust that I can keep us safe. Keep you safe. This doesn't change anything. He won't touch a single hair on your head, Ria."

Ria's arms fall to her sides as she leans into my hold, her cheek turning to rest on my chest.

I turn the stove off and turn her in my arms. I wrap my palms around her cheeks and my thumbs gently brush her tears away.

"I am so sorry, Noah." Her words come out wobbly as she fights against the current of tears streaming down her cheeks.

She bites her lip, fighting to control her emotions.

Using my thumb, I ease her bottom lip out from under her teeth and try a reassuring smile. No matter how I feel, making sure she's okay is my number one priority.

"Baby, listen to me." I tip her chin up so I can meet her eyes. "None of this is your fault. It doesn't matter that this man is your father. You know why?"

She shakes her head once, her teeth pulling at her bottom lip again, in an attempt to stop herself from crying. I gently pull her lip loose and press a gentle kiss on her rosy lips.

"Because he has no claim on you. Never has, so he never will."

I give her another kiss, this time on her jaw as I slant her face ever so slightly to give me better access to her neck.

"I, on the other hand, claim you."

I kiss the hollow of her neck right below her ear, and I feel her shiver at my touch.

"I am your husband. You are my wife. You are mine just as much as I am yours."

I bite her earlobe and then blow on it before giving it another gentle tug with my teeth.

"I protect what's mine."

Her eyes flutter close and she gasps softly.

Ria is practically melting in my arms and the emptiness that's been chasing me ceases to exist. The heat radiating off her body finds its way to mine, making me forget everything and everyone else but her.

The earth stands still, like it always does with her. My feet plant themselves firmly on the ground. I no longer feel off center, and as it's always been with her, I forget where I begin and she ends.

The fact that she's letting me hold her like this, kiss her like this? It strengthens my resolve.

This woman is mine.

And at this moment, she believes it. That's all the encouragement I need.

The only thing that matters to me is being with my wife tonight. I want to care for her like I've failed to do so before.

My other hand drops to the back of her knees and I lift her. Gently setting her on the counter, I graze my lips on the curve of her jaw.

"Sit."

I start to turn towards the stove when she reaches out to me and I still, not wanting to break the spell. My eyes find hers and words fail me.

She's looking at me like she used to do. Her eyes holding the promise of forever yet with a twinge of fear that it may not be enough time. My heart leaps to my throat and I struggle to catch my breath.

For over a year I've thought about her like this. For the last month, I've been worried and terrified that she will never look at me like this again.

She looks like the Ria who threw herself in my arms knowing I'd catch her then drove halfway across the country fueled only by trust and faith. *In me*.

Like the Ria who knocked on my door a month later with a packed suitcase and a grin, telling me she loved me for the first time and she was ready to start a life together.

She looked at me with the same softness when she stood at my graduation telling me she was proud of me.

Like the Ria who held my hand and my gaze through the entirety of our small wedding in our backyard, whispering yes to forever.

Just Ria.
My Ria.

Ria

I'm a mess.

I just found out a man wanted by the FBI, who has been stalking me for years, is my father.

But at this moment, I can't make myself care about anything else besides Noah.

I'm sitting here, right now, staring at my beautiful husband who owns my heart.

So much time was taken from us—stolen by the very people he trusted with his life.

And yet, he stands here, determined to do just about anything for me.

For his son.

Somehow, deep down, I know I will lose in the end.

If this is all the time I have with him, I'm taking it.

If there was anything this whole ordeal has taught me, it's that time is precious. I'll be damned if I waste any more.

My fingers graze his shirt and for a moment, I let my eyes drift all over Noah. I selfishly soak in the sight of him, so lucky to have found him and have had the privilege of calling him mine.

Two steps. That's all it takes for him to move between my legs. My face drowns in his palms, while his thumbs caress my cheeks.

"Noah…" His eyes smile gently down at me. "I need you."

My husband stills, and then his forehead presses against mine. His breath fans my face, his voice gruff with need. "I feel like I've been waiting forever to hear you say that again."

My heart beats painfully against my chest, knowing this may very well be the last time. I've wasted weeks being scared, but I know the thing I'm most afraid of is being without him.

I love this man. I love him with everything I am.

Even when we were apart, there wasn't a single second where I regretted taking a risk on him.

A flood of emotions threatens to pull me under, but I hold on to him like a life raft.

My arms come around his shoulders and my fingers thread into his brown locks.

I pull him closer, and with a low growl, he closes the last few inches between us.

I'll drown on my own time, because right now, I want to lose myself in this moment with him. This is what will keep me going later on when we're apart and I'm missing him.

At least we'll have tonight.

We'll have this. *This goodbye.*

Noah

I see it in her eyes.
 Under the need, lies the finality of tonight.
She's saying goodbye, and so I let her.

Noah

I ease Ria gently onto the pillow, pulling my arm out from under her neck. I position two more pillows on either side of her, tucking the covers under her chin.

I allow myself a few extra minutes to take her in. She's wearing my shirt; the same one she wore that first night, all those years ago. My stomach dips at the memory.

A cement block is resting heavily on my chest, causing a sharp pain in my heart. My fear intensifies with each second. We're still here, knowing there's a chance we could be ambushed at any given time.

I brush a kiss on her shoulder, breathing in her scent for a moment, and she stirs.

"Noah?" Her sleepy whisper is my undoing.

"I'm sorry, baby... I didn't mean to wake you. I need to check and make sure everything is going according to plan, okay? Get some rest and I'll come get you when it's time."

Her hand comes up to cup my cheek and she strokes my jaw. "Thank you."

She rises and I meet her halfway.

We let ourselves indulge in a slow, fervent kiss.

I feel her smile against my lips as she pulls away.

I'm about to lean in and steal another when a knock pulls us apart.

I spring to my feet, looking over my shoulder to check that the noise didn't rouse Adrian.

Ria moves out of bed to go check on him.

I pull open the door to find Gabe standing in the hallway, a grim look on his face.

"You were right."

Fuck.

I squeeze my hands into fists and have to remind myself that my very scared wife and sleeping son are in the same room.

I turn to tell Ria I'll be right back when she comes up to us.

Adrian is sucking on a bottle in her arms.

"What's going on? What were you right about?"

It takes all the strength I have to unclench my fists.

I wanted to spare her this detail, because I have a feeling it may make her spiral into a panic.

I share a look with Gabe and he simply shakes his head at me. He's done keeping secrets from her, and I can tell by the way his jaw is locked that he feels the betrayal as much as I do.

In the end, the mole turned out to be the same man who kept me away from my family and ordered my best friend to do his dirty work for him.

He took orders from a traitor.

Director Villegas.

∼

WE'RE BACK in the basement less than an hour later.

The three agents posted at the house are now packing everything up in our bedroom.

I wasn't letting my family out of my sight now after learning about my former boss.

IN CASE YOU DIDN'T KNOW

The basement is the only safe space within the four walls of the cabin, and it took very little coaxing to get Ria down here.

Turns out, Ria never trusted Villegas.

As soon as we found out Patty and CJ's drop off was made in Texas while I was still there, my suspicions started building.

I needed to be sure before bringing it up, so I had Mina compile a list of all the cities and states the Director assigned me to, and compare it with the dates of drop offs.

Every single date matched. Every single drop off was made where I was posted.

It was as if he actively built a case against me, setting me up to take the fall for Santos.

Once Mina made the connection, it didn't take much coercion to get Ben to do some digging on the Director. They were both as invested in this as Gabe and I were. Ben now had enough evidence to confirm that Villegas was getting paid by a private company owned by a Vincent *Santos*. Finally putting a name to the notorious leader of Sotnas, we were able to do a more thorough search. Ben found several offshore accounts, and from there, he was able to trace the connection between Santos and several cartels all over the world.

Now, our focus is getting the hell out of here.

"*Ria.*" Gabe's clipped tone draws my attention.

Mina and I are mapping out an escape route while Ben works on wiping our digital footprint.

We're on our own now.

Gabe stalks to the monitors, his hands shoving through his hair as he watches our backup at work. To say he's antsy and pissed is an understatement. His hands flex over his gun and I know if we come across Villegas, Gabe will have him on his ass in seconds.

Ria hugs Adrian tight across her chest, unease written all over her. She stares at Gabe, waiting for him to continue.

His words come out in an exhale as he drags out every word.

"I know that I have extinguished any hope of you ever trusting me again, but I need you to understand this is for Adrian's safety. Given we don't even know the difference between friend or foe outside these four walls, I see no other way that will ensure he's protected."

I drop the map I'm holding and stride across the room to stand next to my wife.

"What are you talking about, Reyes?"

Gabe looks over at Ben as if asking for assistance, and then it clicks when I meet Mina's eyes.

Mina sighs and approaches us cautiously, pointing her thumbs over at the monitors behind her.

"We need a diversion, in case someone out there is working with Villegas and feeding him intel."

My eyes glaze over with rage, just thinking of my boss. If Gabe doesn't get to him first, my gun will.

I nod my head and motion for her to continue.

But this time, Ben speaks up. "I didn't have time to do more than an initial background check on anyone, but I think it's safe to assume Villegas has at least one mole working for him on our team."

I grit my teeth in annoyance. Why won't they just get to the point?

With a grunt, Gabe moves to stand in front of us.

"I think it's also safe to assume that Santos knows about Adrian."

A squeak comes out of Ria as she visibly shudders, pulling Adrian even closer. She rests her cheek on Adrian's head, silent tears spilling down her cheeks.

Then it clicks.

"You want to split up."

I mentally switch to agent mode as I try my best to quiet the voice inside me, screaming that I'm also a husband and a dad.

Carefully minding his tone, Gabe stares straight at Ria as he drops the bomb I know will crush her.

"Ben and Mina will take Adrian, while Noah and I protect you."

Ria's head swings to me, eyes wild and crazed, betrayal marring her features.

"NO! Noah has to stay with Adrian." Her hand comes to clutch my bicep. "Tell them, Noah. You promised me. YOU PROMISED!"

I rub my hand over my face, trying to figure how I can explain this to her.

I'm not thrilled about this either.

Adrian is my son.

I've already lost so much time with him, never even getting to see his birth or important firsts.

The fact that I can't be there to protect him guts me. But this...this is what we have to do.

"Ria. Listen to me. Really listen, okay? I get it. You want Adrian protected. We all do. But Santos will stop at nothing to get to the both of us. Villegas has been setting me up to take the fall. And we have evidence that Santos wants me dead. If I take Adrian, none of us will be safe. He will find you and still go after me. But if Mina and Ben take Adrian, there is a much bigger chance of keeping Adrian safe and undiscovered--"

Ria drops to her knees, sobbing. Her cries come out low and strangled. Adrian starts fussing in her arms. I crouch down beside her, gathering my son in one arm while I cradle my wife in the other.

My shoulders shake from the intense pain crowding my chest.

I don't even care that I'm crying in front of my colleagues.

This is my family, for fuck's sake.

My wife. My son.

"Ria…"

"I know."

Ria

Everything happens so fast.

Gabe gave us as much time as possible to say goodbye to Adrian, but before I could even wipe all my tears away, I was ushered upstairs by Noah.

Every minute we spend here is a minute that he--my father--gets closer to finding us here.

I get why the rush is necessary, but it didn't make it any easier for me to handle.

Something happens to you when you're a mother separated from your child.

Like a part of your soul gets sucked out, and you lose the best parts of yourself.

On the outside, I remain calm and portray a mask of indifference but on the inside my heart is bursting into tiny fragments that can never be put back together again.

For the first time since I had Adrian, we would be apart.

I was moving before I even had time to think things through, and I feel every painful beat of my heart.

I'm barely holding it in as I carry Adrian's car seat to the blacked-out SUV waiting for us just outside the cabin. It takes every ounce of energy I have not to drag my feet or look over my shoulder.

"Let's just get to the car, baby... then you can let go, okay? Just hang in there."

Noah's not faring any better. I can tell very little would set him off. His hold on the small of my back tightens as he leads me to the car. I can see his other hand clenching his side, like at any moment, he'll shoot anyone who dares look at me.

I know my husband better than I know myself.

His heart is breaking.

The intensity of his pain has sharpened the angles of his face.

There's a storm brewing behind his eyes that's almost visceral.

Once we get to the car, Noah turns to shield me with his body as I get in the car. I'm buckling in the empty car seat while Noah shuts the door behind him.

He quickly rounds the car to the passenger seat while Gabe stands by my door, waiting for Noah to enter the car.

My husband steals a look, his face impassive like mine, but the light in his eyes from last night has diminished, replaced with rage. I try my best to give him a smile, but Gabe starts the car and my tears start flowing again.

"It's okay, Ree... You can let go."

I look out the window at the place I called my refuge for over a year.

An overwhelming number of emotions keep a tight grip on my heart as the cabin gets smaller.

We drive away and the view of it disappears.

My heart escapes, and I leave it behind with my son.

"Let's go over the plan again," Noah barks at Gabe, raw emotion coating his voice as he looks over his shoulder briefly at me. His weapon rests on his knee.

The plan is to have the standby team support our departure, while Mina and Ben hang back to clear the basement. As soon as the agents clear out, they will make their escape with Adrian in the Ford Explorer at the back of the cabin.

Saying goodbye to Mina was bittersweet but I carry with me the knowledge that my son is in good hands with her and Ben.

Gabe, Noah, and I will drive towards the new safe house Villegas has set up for us. As soon as we cross state lines, Gabe will shake the support team that's tailing us, with the help of his DEA contact. That contact will be waiting for us at an undisclosed location with his own backup team, creating a diversion so we can escape quickly.

Our hope is to get to that point safely, without getting intercepted or derailed by Santos and his cohorts. Then we'll head to the DEA office until we can get everything in place to finally nab Santos, Villegas and the rest of Sotnas.

All *I* can do is hope and pray that Adrian stays protected, and at the end of this that Noah can get to him safely.

Noah

Shortly after leaving the cabin, rain followed, leaving us in a flurry of mist.

We are racing against time we can't waste as the rain continues, even hours later. I hazard another look at my wife, who finally stopped crying, and has now switched to staring blindly out the window with a hand clutching her stomach. I can feel the intensity of her pain as if it were my own, and I wish, not for the first time, that I could steal away every ounce of it.

Beside me, Gabe swiftly glances at the rear-view mirror and the sudden movement pulls me back to the situation at hand.

Stay on task, Noah.
Keep Ria safe.
Bring down Sotnas.
Then, get to Adrian.
Simple enough.

"Noah." There's an edge to Gabe's tone, breaking me out of my reverie.

I look back at him and notice his grip has tightened on the steering wheel.

My eyes quickly snap to the side mirror, and I notice what has him on edge.

"How long?"

Gabe clucks his tongue as he presses lightly on the gas to increase our speed.

"Fifteen minutes."

"How many? And when?"

"I counted three about ten miles back, then another three cars exited at five."

"How far are we to POC?"

"Point of contact is still thirty miles away."

"Shit." I unbuckle my seatbelt and reach for the 9mm pistol resting on my knee. I shift in my seat to quickly grab Gabe's weapon and slide it on the dash for him.

Turning in my seat, I glance over at Ria who somehow has a Glock in her hand. My eyes roam the backseat and that's when I see her pant leg pulled up.

"Ria--"

"Not a word, Noah. You gave me enough lessons over the years, not to mention the ones Mina gave me. I know how to shoot a gun, and trust me, with the way I feel right now? I need to shoot someone."

Fuck.

"You don't--"

"Yes, I do. I want to help protect us."

I nod my head grimly, looking away to check our tail. "The car is bulletproof."

"I hope theirs isn't."

My head whips back. She isn't looking at me anymore. She's unbuckled herself and is looking over her shoulder to the back.

"Just let her," Gabe quietly whispers, low enough for only me to hear.

I don't get time to process the change in my wife because suddenly the explosive sound of multiple guns discharging fills the air.

"Sunroof!" Gabe's foot thumps the gas and we speed off,

letting our support team engage with enemy fire. I quickly push my back against my seat, lowering it enough to slide over to the back with Ria.

With an arm around her, I press her down on the seat. "Stay down, Ria."

I stick my gun back inside the holster inside my pant leg and grab one of the M4s Mina had stashed in the backseat.

"I'm going up there, okay? Just please don't do anything."

I give her a swift kiss on the forehead and hand her some loaded magazines.

"When I give you the signal Ree, hand me a new one, okay?"

Gabe opens the sunroof and I pop out of it, keeping my eyes trained on the shootout in front of me. From the tally Gabe has been taking and my count, our team managed to take two of their cars out, but three of ours are down for the count. That leaves only five teams trailing us, protecting us.

No sooner had I trained my weapon to shoot at the closest car, that a Jeep pulls up with two men coming out on either side, armed with AR-15s.

I pull back the rod, releasing the handle and engaging the safety catch.

I crack my neck and aim straight for the driver.

Shooting a round at my target, I then aim for the car right behind them and fire off another round.

Both cars swivel around before the car behind slams into the tail end of the Jeep, causing it to hit the rail and go off the bridge into the water below.

The car behind rights itself as the driver's door opens and the body of the driver is shoved out onto the freeway. Two more heads pop out and a round of rapid gunfire fills the air.

A tint of green grabs my attention.

"Pump the gas, Reyes! Grenade incoming!"

Gabe slams on the gas, causing me to jolt forward as a bullet barely misses my ear by an inch.

Two of our cars explode in a blaze of fire in front of me.

We're down to three cars each.

And who knows how many they have trailing behind, poised at the ready.

I take the moment of camouflage to reach inside the car and Ria hands me another round. As soon as I load, I aim for the heads sticking out of the armored cars driving past the wreckage, and I unload on them.

A groan of satisfaction escapes me as sweat pours down my face.. The intense heat from the multiple fires blazing on the freeway has me burning up, and the Kevlar underneath my clothes is not helping matters. But I focus on sweeping the scene as it unfolds in front of me in a flurry of red smoke and rapid gunshots. I stick my hand back into the car to ask for a reload.

Smacking the magazine in, my eyes survey the damage. As quickly as fear had left me, it comes raging back when I spot the two armored cars entering the freeway.

I slide back into the car, my chest heaving. My breath shudders and I struggle to release it.

Gabe eyes me from the rearview mirror, and from his vantage point, I know he's already spotted the armored cars catching up to us. I fight like hell to maintain my composure, trying my best to come up with a solid plan to get us out of here.

Beside me Ria is on her haunches, hands planted on the back of her seat. She watches in fear as the enemy flanks us from both sides.

Ria

How can I still be living the same day when so much has happened?

For the briefest of moments, I was filled with the hope that we would get out of this... battle unscathed, but in the blink of an eye, we're surrounded.

And if the grim look on Noah's face is any indication, we're screwed.

Beside me, he engages in a silent conversation with Gabe. Then he swivels, grabbing a bag from the back and pulling out a grenade.

He looks up at me with a grimace as he hands it to me. "Last resort. If they aim for us, Ria, I need you to throw that out your window and duck down to protect yourself. Do you hear me?"

I nod, then watch in horror as he climbs out onto the roof again.

Whereas before the enemy was at least thirty to fifty feet away from us, now their cars were nearly aligned with ours.

I already know they had no qualms about wanting my husband dead, but he is putting himself in the line of fire right in front of me. He is undoubtedly good at his job, but he is still my husband and a father.

I pull on his leg. "Noah! The car is bulletproof but you're not. Get down here."

He ignores me as he starts blasting his rifle. I've never seen Noah in action before and the sight of him in his element is both incredibly appealing and terrifying.

The ham and cheese sandwich Noah forced me to eat a few hours ago threatens to make a reappearance as my stomach rolls over and sweat prickles the back of my neck.

My lungs feel tight and my heart slams against my chest, fighting to get out to wrap itself around the man who owns it.

I watch the open sunroof with bated breath as he changes the magazine out so fast, I nearly miss it.

Instead of aiming at the cars or the heads poking out , he trains his gun at the tires. An explosion drowns out the sounds of gunfire, and cars whip around.

I claw my seat as I raise my head to see over the backseat. Noah has effortlessly blown out all four tires of one of the armored cars. It screeches and Gabe smoothly maneuvers our car out of the way as it misses us and heads straight for the bank two feet behind us, blocking half of the freeway. The remaining cars blast and smash their way through it, causing fragments and bodies to go flying across the interstate.

A bloodcurdling scream reverberates inside the car.

It takes me a second to realize it came from me as I shake from the tremors of what I just witnessed.

I'm suddenly hauled back into my seat and Noah's face is blurry when it comes into my line of sight. I realize I'm crying and screaming, my throat hoarse, and he cups my face.

"Ria, baby. Gabe and I know what we're doing, okay? I can't keep checking on you like this. You can't pull my leg and stop me either. This is my job. Let me work on getting us out of here. Stay down please, and Ree? Whatever you do, keep your eyes shut. Don't look anymore."

He grabs the three magazines I have left in my hands and gently pushes me down onto the floor of the car. With one last lingering look and a peck on the nose, he's back up again.

"Noah is the best of the best, Ria. He knows how to keep himself safe while taking a target down. Just do what he says. The last thing we need is a distracted sniper."

Gabe's gruff voice rattles my insides.

I get it. I really do. I've become one of those annoying 'damsels in distress' in action movies—the ones we scream and yell obscenities at.

I curl my hands into fists on my knees and focus on my breathing until it becomes even. I use every ounce of strength left in me to summon my memories.

The same day I showed up at Noah's apartment and agreed to live with him, he signed me up for classes. He knew there might come a day when someone would target me.

I took classes for everything including judo, taekwondo, and self-defense. He also personally trained me to handle guns. If he tossed me that M4 right now, I could easily clear and disassemble it in three minutes. I wouldn't be able to shoot a target as easily as he or Mina could, but I can definitely protect myself if it comes down to it.

I just need to get out of my head and pretend I'm watching one of those police procedurals I love so much. I need to disassociate from the fact that this is very much real.

My worst nightmare has suddenly become my reality.

With one last huff of breath, I open my eyes, just in time to feel the car spin on its axis.

Noah falls back into the car with a heavy thud. He reaches for me, but the velocity of the car spinning has him smacking his head on the window opposite me.

His eyes glaze over as he stares blindly at me, his hands desperately stretching to grab hold of some part of me before they flutter close with a groan. I gasp in utter terror when his body goes limp, and I notice the pool of blood on his shoulder.

"GABE! Gabe! Noah got shot!"

I have to shut my eyes as I'm hit with a rush of vertigo so intense, I nearly lose that sandwich.

The car stops spinning but continues to careen sideways. I scream for Gabe to help me but when he refuses to answer, I arch my back and forcefully squeeze my way out of my spot on the car floor.

I'm grasping Noah's arm when my eyes stray to the front.

Gabe is sprawled out on the dashboard with his cheek pressed to the steering wheel.

The window is cracked on the driver side and there's blood gushing out of his forehead from where he hit his head.

One of them might be dead, and I barely begin to process that thought when the car screeches to a stop, causing me to fly back on to my side of the backseat.

The gun I had been clutching falls from my hands and slides underneath the seat next to Noah.

With a strangled cry, I crawl back towards Noah, determined to wake him up so we can get out of here, when I see movement in my peripheral.

I scream Noah's name over and over again, patting his knee and hoping he will wake up before they manage to get in.

Grabbing the grenade he tossed me, I shove it into my bra.

I kick Noah's leg and he stirs but doesn't wake up.

I'm about to grab his arm again when my door is pried open and I'm hauled out of the car.

I'm kicking and screaming, desperately trying to fight my way back to my husband.

I shove my elbow into the assailant's gut, slamming my heel on his foot.

In return, he knocks me down to my knees as he folds over in pain.

I scramble back up and run towards the car.

Someone yells at me, but my eyes never stray from Noah's lifeless body.

An arm comes around my neck and I'm being choked from behind when yet another voice calls out for me not to be harmed. As soon as the arm relaxes around my neck, I bite down hard.

I'm plopped back down on the ground as I hear the yelps of pain from my attacker.

I grab the grenade I stuffed in my bra, unclipping the pin and tossing it behind me as I push myself to run towards the car.

A loud booming sound fills the air, and the force of the grenade's blast causes me to hurl forward, nearly hitting my head on the freeway.

I attempt to crawl my way back to Noah.

It seems like they might not hurt me, but they will hurt him.

I need to get to him.

I can't leave him here. I can't lose him.

Adrian can't lose his father. Not now that they've finally found their way to each other.

"Noah! Wake up! Please wake up!"

Please wake up.

I push myself to my feet, nearly toppling over from the effects of the blast.

Fires blaze all around me and a rush of vertigo once again threatens me, but I fight through it.

I'm swaying on my feet and my hand goes up to shield my nose as I sputter from the smoke permeating the air.

I'm a few feet from the car when a masked gunman, at least a foot taller than I am, blocks my way. I aim for his groin area but miss when someone else grabs me from behind.

I struggle against the rope they're now tying around my arms, but they flip me onto my back, and I lose the battle as they tie my legs too.

Tears gush out of me as I arch my back, enough for me to see that a few armed men are approaching the car where Gabe and Noah lay unconscious.

"NOAH!"

A white cloth is suddenly shoved into my line of sight, blocking me from seeing what's happening. Before I can yell for either one of them again, the smell of chloroform fills my nasal passages, and everything goes dark.

Noah

RIA!
I awaken to the sound of Ria screaming my name ringing in my head.

Instantly, my skin prickles with awareness.

Ria.

Leaving Adrian.

My son.

Leaving Nebraska.

Gabe swerving to avoid a wayward car skidding across the interstate.

The windshield getting struck by debris, and the impact causing the car to spin out of control.

Tires blowing out.

Falling back inside the car and a bullet grazes my shoulder.

Gabe.

I see Gabe sprawled out on the driver seat, blood all over his face.

That's when it hit me. I passed out.

Adrenaline rushes through me, and I let my senses take over as I mentally break down what I'm up against.

Feel. Smell. Sound. Sight.

My cheek is pressed to a cold, dank cement floor and I've been freed of my weapons.

IN CASE YOU DIDN'T KNOW

My shoulder, chest and ankle holsters are all empty.

There's a slight twinge of pain in my shoulder, but it's bearable.

The graze of a bullet. I've had worse—it barely touched my skin.

A mixture of smells fills the air, combining with the sound of heavy breathing.

My hands are tied behind my back and I almost snicker in disbelief.

They tied me up in rope. *Rope.*

My fucking legs aren't even bound.

I crack one eye open and take in my surroundings, making a mental tally of at least fifteen people all around me.

I can't see behind me, but I clock two men posted at every corner of what looks like an abandoned warehouse.

All armed.

Three tables line the walls with what looks like various drugs, which are being packaged by young women.

Maniac.

These women can't be more than twenty years old.

They are unarmed and obviously terrified.

I hear a muffled sound, feeling her before I see her.

I stumble to my knees and look over my shoulder, only to find Ria bound and gagged on a wicker chair. She's staring straight at me with relief in her eyes, ignoring CJ, who's sitting right beside her with his legs crossed in front of him and a gun resting between his knees.

He's staring at me too, a malevolent smirk on his face. His hand hovers over his weapon.

The coward won't do shit unless ordered. That much is obvious.

I turn my focus back to my wife.

Her black hair is in disarray and plastered to her face. Dirt and blood streak her face, caking her arms. Her clothes are torn in various places and there's blood splatter and grime all over her.

I know, without a doubt, my girl put up a fight.

Are you okay? I mouth the words to her, wishing I could just toss her over my shoulder and run.

Her eyes are rimmed with red and she nods faintly to me, flinching when her attention is caught by something over my shoulder.

I straighten and turn my eyes upward. I spot Director Villegas, followed by the elusive man himself.

Vincent Santos.

They're making the descent down through a spiral staircase in the middle of the room.

I let my eyes wander behind them to quickly take in a possible escape route, and I see the door they left open. *A way out.*

Through there is another door. I can just make out what looks to be a parking lot, right next to a body of water.

I tear my eyes away as their footsteps near the last stair. The last thing I need is them knowing I've scoped out a point of escape.

As they come around the bend of the staircase, they sport identical smug expressions.

Santos pauses as his eyes flicker behind me to Ria.

He growls and yells a curse in what I recognize as Tagalog, gesturing wildly at Ria.

"Mga inutil! Bakit niyo siya tinali? At bakit ganyan ang itsura niya?"

Then, Santos snaps his head towards CJ.

"Untie her!" Santos roars.

CJ jumps forward to free Ria from her constraints, but the force of it causes her to fall off her chair. She drops onto her hands and knees with a sharp gasp, triggering another string of violent, incoherent words that sound like slurs from Santos.

"Dalhin niyo sa akin ang traydor!"

His men rush in from all corners of the room.

One hauls CJ to Santos, forcing CJ down on his knees while the other grabs hold of Ria rather forcefully, causing her to cry out in pain again.

I'm barreling towards him before I'm even aware of it.

I knock him down with my shoulder, ramming his head with my elbow as hard as I can while bound, and then I knee him in the solar plexus for good measure.

Santos' men flank me but stop approaching when Ria flings her body on to me, a petrified look on her face.

She wraps her arms around my waist, burying her face on my chest.

"STOP!" Santos bellows with a hand raised.

His men halt, waiting for his orders.

My chest is heaving but I don't take my eyes off of Santos. He eyes me with disdain before his lips turn upward, calling out to his daughter.

"Alessandria."

Santos' tone oozes with tension as he approaches us.

Ria trembles and I try my best to shield her with my shoulder. My hands are still bound, but I've loosened the rope enough that anyone who tries to grab my wife will get a fist to the face.

"What do you want?" I grit out.

I force myself to stand still, not making a move to pummel this madman to the ground.

He ignores me, his eyes trained on Ria like my wife is *his property*.

"Look at me, Alessandria."

Ria raises her head, eyes meeting mine for a split second.

I catch the trepidation in them before she turns her whole body to meet the man she came from.

The man who wants to steal her away and kill me.

"Hello, sperm donor."

Ria's choice of words causes an evil smirk to line Santos' face. He's proud of the fire in Ria, and not at all surprised she's figured out her connection to him.

"Nice to meet you too, daughter. Excuse me for one second." He turns to one of his men, snaps his finger and then holds out a hand. Before I can blink, one of his men hands him a Glock, which he points straight at CJ.

"Why?" CJ's look of disbelief only causes Santos to sneer.

"You didn't actually think I would let you get away with what you tried to do to her, did you?"

An ear-splitting screech of terror leaves CJ, seconds before Santos shoots him point blank between the eyes.

His body falls on the ground with a thud.

Without any ounce of remorse, Santos tosses the gun on one of the tables, just barely missing one of the packer's heads.

With his lip curled in satisfaction, he turns back to face his daughter.

I've made a mental note of where all weapons are at this point, but I highly doubt he would toss a loaded gun so callously like that.

Which means that gun was loaded with exactly one bullet.

This reeks of premeditation.

He planned to dispose of CJ in front of Ria all along.

Out of the corner of my eye, I spot CJ's discarded weapon under the sink where he dropped it in his haste to untie Ria.

Behind Santos, three of his men haul CJ's lifeless body up to the far right corner of the dingy basement where the wall curves and disappears. Another pair picks up the thug who manhandled Ria and follow suit.

I hear a door open a few clicks later, then another shortly after that, leading me to believe this place has more doorways and halls. More points of exit.

My eyes track the room.

Ten people are left in the room: five armed men, including Santos and Villegas, three unarmed female packers, Ria and myself.

The odds of disarming all five on my own are high, but not without bloodshed or the possibility of people getting hurt.

"Now that we've gotten rid of the trash, let's move on to the 'getting to know each other' part of this reunion, shall we?" Santos stares at Ria like a lion hunting a lamb. "You must have something to say to your dear old daddy."

Ria tenses beside me, as she actively avoids looking at her father. Her body language screams discomfort, and I know she's trying to scrub the image of CJ from her brain.

"I have nothing to say to you."

Tension sparks across the room, radiating from everyone who is anxiously listening to this back and forth.

Santos' guards take an offensive stance, like they're waiting for a command.

My eyes stray to my former boss.

He's paler than I've ever seen him, not even bothering to hide the terror written all over his face. It's like he's anticipating Santos training a gun at his face for failing to accomplish what he was paid to do.

I turn my attention back to Santos, who has gone eerily silent.

I watch as he rakes his eyes up and down Ria before his gaze finally lands back on me. A shadow crosses his face, and

I watch in satisfaction as his expression turns almost lethal when he sees the protective way Ria is holding onto me.

If she's in the way, he won't dare hurt me.

The fact that she's willing to risk her life for me pisses him off.

I have no idea if the tracker Ben put on me is still on, but I hope these amateurs didn't find it so Ben can track us and alert the DEA. We've already mapped out a secondary plan, should we get ambushed. Ben should have been actively tracking us this entire time. If we even slightly veered off track, he wouldn't hesitate to call in the cavalry.

I need to remain calm and buy us enough time.

And I need to do that without provoking Santos, who clearly wants me dead.

Ria

He's pissed.

My father is beyond livid, judging by the tic in his jaw and the way his eyes, the ones that look exactly like mine, blaze as they zero in on my hand gripping Noah's waist.

It's been close to thirty years since the photo of him and my mom was taken, but the years have been kind to him. Maybe his money plays a part in that, because aside from the slight wrinkles on his forehead, he does not appear to have aged much.

The only difference is his vibe, his whole aura has a sinister edge to it.

This man is not kind at all. He reeks of power, money, and the blood he must leave in his wake whenever someone crosses him.

I can tell he doesn't like it when things don't go according to plan.

And more importantly, Noah being here is the last thing he anticipated or wanted.

After all these years, my father finally wants me around. If I weren't hanging on to Noah right now, he would have had his men take care of my husband the way he just took care of CJ.

Shifting his gaze away, Santos makes a show of pacing the

room, stopping by a table where women––*girls,* are packing drugs.

Their movements falter as Santos bends down to inspect their work.

He's on edge, and he's going to take it out on these innocent young women.

Noah shifts beside me, his eyes narrowing when he notices the sudden shift in the air.

My stomach recoils with disgust at the thought of being related to someone this blatantly cruel.

Against my better judgment, I open my mouth to interrupt his perusal.

I'll never forget watching CJ die. I already foresee nightmares in my future. I won't let him hurt these girls, too.

"What do you want from me, *father*––" I spit the words out, my nails biting into my palms.

He spins around, still holding the little baggy, satisfaction etching the lines on his forehead and around his eyes. It makes him appear even more sinister.

He *was* baiting me, and he's damn near giddy that I took it.

"You're my daughter."

He tosses the bag callously back on the table and then snaps his fingers, pointing at the three women. My insides twist, seeing the way they don't even need to hear the words to know that they're being dismissed.

They scamper to their feet like mice, one of them nearly tripping over her feet as she rushes out the door in obvious relief. As I watch them leave, I spot CJ's gun on the floor. The memory of CJ running the barrel over my face as he threatened to kill Noah has goosebumps rising on my skin.

I feel Noah look down at me, a crease between his eyebrows, and I work on keeping a straight face. I nearly forgot how attuned he is to me.

I muster enough courage to voice the question I'm not really sure I want to hear the answer to.

"Why now?"

I force myself to meet Santos' gaze, and I'm rewarded when his lip curls in what I'm guessing is his best attempt at a smile.

"Why not now?"

My hand curls around Noah's shirt and I feel him tense beside me.

I open my mouth to speak, deciding against it. If anything, it will edge him further to another fit of fury and Noah could get hurt.

Instead, I raise an eyebrow at Santos and wait.

I relax my arm around Noah, pretending I'm simply moving my hands to cross them on my chest. I let my fingers linger on Noah's back, subtly tugging the rope binding his hands.

I bite back my smile when I find it's already looser than it should be.

Of course my husband knows how to untie himself.

Crossing my arms, I face Santos.

I stop myself from tapping my foot but I put on a mask of indifference for good measure, just to see the fire burn brighter in his eyes.

What did Mom see in this guy?

He's a somewhat attractive guy, but I feel the evil practically emanating from him. He's vibrating with it.

"What are you thinking about so seriously over there, Alessandria?"

I bristle, and the words are out of my mouth before I can stop them.

"Just seriously wondering what my mom ever saw in you."

An ominous chuckle leaves his mouth and displeasure is evident on his face.

I can almost hear the groan Noah stifles as he shifts his shoulder, blocking part of me from Santos. I frown and side-step so I'm in front of him, my body shielding his.

He may be a federal agent, but I'm this criminal's daughter.

He won't hurt me.

"Easy, baby." Noah leans over, his breathy whisper hot on my neck, and memories of being together last night rush through me.

My father glowers at us, his distaste with Noah so clearly written on his face.

He directs his gaze across the room to Villegas, nodding his head.

"Bring them in."

Noah's boss disappears into a room directly across from us, and when he reenters the room, he's no longer alone. The shock causes me to take a step towards them, but the matching scowls plastered on Penelope and Aunt Patty's faces stop me in my tracks.

"Hello, Alessandria." The disdain dripping in Penny's voice can't be missed. She tucks a wayward strand of hair behind her ear and shoots me an icy glare.

Santos clears his throat and I flick a glance towards him, my confusion evident.

Irritation is written all over his face as he raises an eyebrow at the two women.

My head swings back and I see Patty compose herself quickly. She nudges Penny, wrapping a hand around her elbow but Penny refuses to budge. I lived with her for years, I can practically recite every facial expression she has ever had based on memory.

This is her 'you're wasting my time' face. She's pissed

she's here, and even more that *I'm* the reason she's here. But there's something else simmering behind her amber eyes.

Hate? Why does she hate me so much?

So many questions build in my head, causing me to ping pong my head back and forth between these two women and my deadbeat criminal of a father.

Ria

"What--why--what is going on?"

My voice wavers, my emotions suddenly overpowering every ounce of effort to remain neutral.

Santos takes that moment to cross the room, not stopping until he reaches Penny.

His hand grips her chin, forcing her to tear her gaze away from mine to his. He snaps his fingers in her face.

"Get that nasty look off of your face, sweetheart, unless you have a death wish."

He whispers the words, but it echoes back into the silence of the room.

I feel my eyes widen as I take a step in their direction.

My father looks over his shoulder at the sound.

"Patience, daughter. You'll get your turn."

He wraps his other hand around the back of Penny's neck, shoving her down on the floor.

"Now kneel like a good little girl and apologize to my daughter."

Aunt Patty gasps and launches herself in front of Penny.

"I'm sorry, Vincent. She's sorry. Please, please don't do this. You promised!"

"Control your daughter then, Patricia."

He sneers down at her, wrenching his gaze away from them.

IN CASE YOU DIDN'T KNOW

"I'm your daughter too!" Penny cries out, her palms slamming into fists on the cement floor.

I stumble back at her words, unable to comprehend what the hell is going on right now.

Everything plays out in slow motion, like a movie I don't want to watch but somehow can't tear my eyes away from.

Tears blur my vision as I stare at Penny, crying and huffing on the floor. She's a mess. Her usually perfectly styled hair is in disarray, her cheeks have dirt on them, and she has tears on her dress.

In all the years I have known her, I never saw a hair out of place. Even when we lived together, she always made sure she was the epitome of perfection.

The only emotion Penny had ever shown me was anger and I never even saw her cry. Not once.

Now, seeing her an emotional heap on the floor is tearing at my will to stay impassive.

"Penny? Are we--are we sisters?"

Penny's head jerks up and she makes a move to get up as if to charge at me, but Aunt Patty physically grabs her from behind to keep her from lunging at me.

My heart drops to my feet and I'm at a loss, my mouth gaping open as she starts yelling obscenities at me.

Ever since we first met, my presence has been a contention between her and Aunt Patty. But knowing it's because we're related? I'm not sure how I'm supposed to process or even begin to understand any of this.

"Will someone please tell me what the hell is going on?"

I stomp my feet in frustration. I'm asking all these questions and no one--not a single person—has answered any of them.

My father remains silent and looks almost *bored* as he stares down at Penny.

The fact that he didn't order anyone to get Penny after

she tried attacking me speaks volumes. He cares about her, to some degree, but is feigning indifference.

"Aunt Patty? Why--why are you here? Did you know who I was this whole time?"

Santos snaps his finger again, his eyes still trained on Penny, who is now hunched over on the floor with her face buried in her hands as she cries. His forehead creases slightly, betraying his indifference.

Director Villegas grabs Aunt Patty's arm and hauls her to her feet.

"My daughter asked you a question, Patricia. Know your place and answer her."

My chest heaves with pressure.

The way he is speaking to them doesn't sit right with me, but at the same time, I'm at such a loss.

I shut my eyes and take a few steps back until I'm once again within the safety of Noah's chest.

My back rests on his front.

I feel every beat of his heart and I let that center me, allowing his presence to calm me.

He is my gravity.

I look up and meet his concerned gaze.

I shake my head.

I know he's aching to wrap his arms around me, but he doesn't want to let them know he's free of his bindings.

Somewhere in that head of his, he's still trying to map out an escape plan.

But somehow... I know it will be futile.

This man is much too powerful.

"Ria..." Aunt Patty's voice breaks into my harried thoughts and I focus on her.

"Why are you here? Did you know who I was this whole time?"

Her gaze flickers between Santos and Penny before she finally addresses me again.

"Yes and no."

She grabs hold of her arm, rubbing it where Villegas had grabbed her.

The fear in her eyes is unmistakable, but there's also a tinge of blame as she glances at me.

"My engagement to Vincent was an arranged one. It was a business deal between our parents to help repay the debt my father owed his father. Shortly after Vincent and I got married... I-I stumbled upon pictures of you as a baby in his study. I questioned him, asking him who you were. In response, he offered an alternative solution to clearing the debt my family owed. My family was still in the process of paying our debts to the Santos family, so Vincent relieved our debts in exchange for watching over your mother." Her gaze turns inward, like she is reliving those moments again.

"Watching over you... I did it without hesitation. I had just found out I was pregnant with Penny, and naturally, I was curious about your mother."

Aunt Patty's eyes flutter close for the briefest of moments before she opens them again, eyes brimming with tears.

"I grew close to Chloe, your mom in that time. She was the sweetest, most kind and trusting person I had ever met. I couldn't wrap my head around how she could have fallen for Vincent, but I understood why he came to love her. I had grown to love her like a sister for those same reasons. But I had to remind myself—she was Vincent's side piece. Whether Chloe knew it back then or not, I didn't care. I had Penny to consider, and it was my job--a job that almost cost me my life."

Anger flashes in her eyes before she remembers who is watching her. She lowers her head as she composes herself and continues.

"Your mom found out about my relationship with Vincent."

She huffs out an irritated breath. "I told her over and over again she didn't need to come to Penny's graduation, but she refused to listen. She came with you in tow. She saw Vincent there and pieced everything together. She stopped updating Vincent on your life causing him to question my loyalty and threaten me. Then your mom, out of sheer spite, moved the both of you and we couldn't find you. It wasn't until we were alerted by the hospital that we learned of your whereabouts because Chloe still had Vincent listed as her emergency contact. And that's when we came up with the Foundation--"

"The foundation?"

She rolls her eyes. "Yes. The foundation. Truthfully, there was never a foundation. It was all me. I paid every single cent you and your mother owed. I took you in and took care of your every need. To this day, I still can't wrap my head around Chloe's actions. I can't believe I fell for your mother's fake persona. She was not the person I thought she was. She didn't deserve any of Vincent's help, yet she had it in spades and still she refused. Your mother decided she was going to be a martyr and instead of accepting help, she had you working your ass off to pay her hospital bills. You were disgustingly thin when I saw you again. What kind of mother does that? She was nothing but a selfish bitch. A whore."

Unknowingly, I had taken steps towards her as she recounted her role in all this.

Once I get to her, my hand goes up of its own volition.

I slap her across the cheek and then my eyes snap to my hand as the sting of the slap burns my palm.

"Don't you dare talk about my mother like that" My voice comes out in a shaky whisper.

Suddenly, Santos gets in between us, his face red with rage.

He grabs the back of Aunt Patty's neck and yanks her forward.

"I thought I told you to never ever speak about her like that, especially in front of my daughter!"

Santos rears back as if to slap her too and involuntarily, my hands go around his arm.

He stills, his eyes boring into mine before they fly to my hands on his arm.

He practically hisses at me, disbelief etched on his face as it battles with the anger simmering behind eyes that look just like mine.

"What do you think you're doing, Alessandria? This--this woman insulted your mother."

I shake my head. "I don't care. Right now, all I care about is knowing the whole story."

I'm angry at him.

So fucking angry.

I want nothing more than to not see him for the rest of my life, but I know that's not an option.

"How about you answer my questions this time? Tell me everything."

With a crook of his eyebrow, he begins to calm down as he turns his attention to me.

He barely spares Aunt Patty a cursory glance before letting her go.

She falls to the floor next to Penny and their arms go around each other.

Santos wipes his hand on his trousers before flicking a glance at Villegas.

He waves a hand toward the sobbing women and snaps his fingers, and before I could even blink, Villegas pulls a gun out and points it straight at them.

I swallow my gasp, afraid that any reaction from me will spur him on.

I fight to remain impassive when all I want to do is get between them and the gun.

I share a look with Noah.

He shakes his head once and his message is clear.

Don't do anything Ria. Don't provoke him.

"Very well, Alessandria."

Santos takes his suit jacket off, hanging it on the chair recently vacated by one of the drug packers.

He rolls his sleeves up and for a man presumably in his fifties, he's pretty fit.

He's got tattoos peeking out from under the sleeves and I notice the same tag that was on CJ's arm.

I attempt to take a discreet step backward closer to Noah and farther from my estranged father, but he notices.

He cracks his neck and his jaw clenches as his eyes meet mine again.

"Before I begin, just remember, daughter, I came here for a reason. I intend to leave here with you in tow. It's time to come home where you belong. So, get that notion that you're somehow leaving with this man out of your head."

Jutting my chin, I match his stance.

I'm ignoring his calling Noah "this man" when he knows that Noah is my husband. I let my anger be my armor.

"Stop avoiding my questions and answer them."

Another chuckle passes his lips, a real smile actually ghosting his face this time.

"Alright. Well, some of what Patricia said was accurate, but then again, I never bothered to correct her. I met your mother before my father decided on this arranged marriage with the Cortez's."

He sighs, rubbing the back of his neck.

"It was my senior year of college and I met Chloe at some

stupid party. At the time, I didn't plan on pursuing anything with anyone, knowing I would be coming home to take over the family business. She was a friend of a friend, but we instantly clicked. We started having meals together, studying together and eventually it progressed. I delayed going back to the Philippines for as long as I could because I fell for your mother."

His gaze roams my face and I know he's remembering my mom when they were young.

"I brought Chloe home with me during that last summer. We went travelling together, and that was when I proposed to her. At the time, I knew she was it for me. But before we got to the Philippines, your grandfather had already made the arrangement with the Cortez's. They had connections that went beyond Asia that our business desperately needed if we wanted to go global. I couldn't very well just walk away when I was the sole heir. But when I explained this to your mother, she wouldn't have it. She had no intention of being--"

He starts tugging at his tie like the words are choking him. "--the other woman. Then, after learning what kind of business the family actually did, she left me. She went back home to America without so much as a backwards glance."

He looks back at me, venom shooting out of his eyes.

"Just like that--like we were never anything more than a passing fling."

He continues to tug at his tie, his agitation starting to break the surface.

"Then she found out about you. We didn't have cellphones or the internet at the time, so she didn't have a way to let me know she was pregnant. When Chloe had you, I wasn't there. I wasn't even aware. I had no say in your doctor or even your last name. She didn't even include me in your birth certificate, taking away any rights I had to even call you mine."

He clucks his tongue, eyes moving past me to Noah. My father rakes his gaze over Noah, shaking his head.

"By the time I learned about you, you were almost a year old. If I had not tried to find your mother, I would never even have found out I was a father."

He removes his tie, his gaze landing on my belly and then my face.

He raises his eyebrow before he turns to look at Aunt Patty on the floor next to him.

That's when I realize: he knows about Adrian.

My eyes fly to Noah, both of us coming to the same conclusion.

Even though we both understand the stakes and what we need to do to ensure Adrian's safety, I know he has a plan.

He's not going to let me go without a fight.

My stomach churns, like a cocktail of fear-induced acid rising up my throat, almost choking me. I struggle to not look like I'm trying to catch my breath as I sneak a look around the room.

The two bodyguards have posted themselves on either side of Villegas. He still has his gun raised at Aunt Patty and Penny, who hold each other while sobbing.

My father is still staring at Aunt Patty, a faraway look in his eyes.

I clear my throat, needing to distract him and needing answers.

"Then what? Why do you suddenly want me around? What do you want from me?"

Santos turns to look at me.

A flicker of pain flashes on his face before he masks it with indifference.

"Make no mistake, daughter. I. Always. Wanted. You. Around." He sounds out every word through gritted teeth.

"But why now? What exactly is my role in all of this?"

He scoffs, like he can't believe I even have the nerve to ask such a dumb question.

"Shortly after we were married, Patty discovered she was pregnant and so I moved her here while I conducted business. But I never forgot about your mother. I hired a private investigator. When the PI finally found Chloe and discovered she had a kid, it didn't take me long to figure out you were mine. It took a lot of coaxing, but your mother finally agreed to meet up with me, but she was no longer the same woman. She didn't want any help. She absolutely didn't want me around you. Around her. I had to beg her to even accept any money. Chloe was struggling. You were living in a shoebox apartment. A fucking studio."

He spits that last part out like the mere idea of living in a normal apartment was abhorrent to him.

"She was a teacher by day, waitress at a club by night. Neighbors babysitting you? Imagine. Your father is one of the wealthiest people on earth and my own flesh and blood is getting babysat by a bunch of factory workers, while the mother of my child whores herself out for tips for diaper money?"

He turns on me suddenly, a hard glint in his eyes. A blush of fury creeps up his neck and he's shaking his head vehemently, now lost in his memories.

"Chloe gave me no choice. The business here was still too green. I could not risk anyone knowing about the both of you, especially not your grandfather or--" He cuts off, his eyes shutting for a moment.

And then it hits me. He was protecting my mother and I from my grandfather.

"So, I made a deal with Patty. It was only supposed to be

until I could get your mother to let me be a part of your life--lives. Then, the business boomed. We expanded to all fifty states, to Asia and Australia, until we dominated the entire globe. But with wealth and power came enemies and constant threats to my family. I knew there would be nothing I could do to protect you and your mother if anyone found out about you so I had to come up with an alias. I needed to cover my tracks and assume a different identity. Patty took over any contact with you and your mother. Then your mother--" His voice cracks as he runs a palm over his face.

"My mom got sick?"

He releases a frustrated breath and nods once as he shares a glance with Aunt Patty. She has managed to calm herself down while my father spun his tale.

"You had just graduated high school. I wanted to support you moving forward, and for a while, Chloe seemed to be on board with it. Then she found out Patty was my wife, and Penny--" He clears his throat, and Penny wails again.

He opens his mouth like he wants to say something, but indecision passes over his face and he twists around to face me again.

Sighing, he continues. "It became harder to get through to her. She was convinced any connection with me would ruin your life. She ran off with you. We eventually found you but your mother refused any help. I consulted with her doctor to find a way to help her but by then, it was too late. Chloe died and you disappeared."

His voice starts rising by octaves.

"I had no idea you were living in motels. I figured you would keep staying at your apartment or downgrade. When I found out your mother had never even attempted to access the money I put in an account for her and you were working yourself to the bone, I knew I couldn't approach you. I had Patty take you in. Then you met--"

His voice takes a volatile tone as he pivots to face Noah once again.

"My husband?"

He snarls like he is disgusted by our relationship and it raises my hackles.

Noah's face is the epitome of fury right now. Like *Dean Winchester* come to life.

He's breathing hard, his jaw flexing.

I shake my head, lost in the weird direction my thoughts took me. I don't notice that Aunt Patty has gotten up with Penny under her arm.

"Up until that moment, I had a plan. I would wait for you to finish college and Patty would introduce us. I would have you work for me, waiting until the perfect time to introduce myself as your father. But alas luck was not on my side, daughter. Of all the men in the world, you just had to fall in love with a self-righteous one. A man with a badge. I could not risk the repercussions had I approached you then. So again, I waited. I believed it was just a matter of time until you grew tired of him, but again you shocked me. You actually married the man."

His hand sweeps the room as he brazenly points at Noah and then at me.

"The man who was assigned to destroy everything I had built for you--your entire life."

His gaze slides over to Penny and her mother and his mask falls. His face warps into disgust as he looks back at the two women.

A memory hits me and that's when it clicks.

"Wait-WAIT." I look at Penny, my gut churning. "You went to Paris to visit your dad after CJ--"

My hand flies to my mouth as the words leave me, remembering how he killed CJ right in front of me.

Penny simply juts out her chin. That typically ever-present

raised eyebrow of hers finally makes an appearance as she eyes me up and down with disdain. I tamp down the urge to squirm.

"I killed the incompetent waste, Penelope." Santos interrupts, smugness coating his words.

Penny's head swings back to Santos and her lower lip quivers, betraying her emotions.

"CJ--CJ is dead? But you swore!"

He sneers, venom dripping from his lips. "You actually think I was going to let him live after what he did to you? To Alessandria?"

"Then why even keep him alive, Daddy?"

Penelope stomps her feet, a lone tear sliding down her cheek.

What could only be described as a roar escapes Santos' lips. Shocked, I drop my hand and watch as he strides back to Penny and grabs her by the arm.

"He betrayed me. He was supposed to protect you and watch over Ria when you left to run our Europe production. Instead, he got greedy."

He waves his hand around again lazily, like he's annoyed he even has to explain this.

"I kept him alive, hoping he would serve as bait for the agent."

He smirks, flicking a glance at Noah. "He hates him almost as much as I do."

Then his pointed gaze returns to Penny as he releases her from his grasp. He wipes his hand down his trousers and Penny starts to wail again.

"Daddy!"

Santos growls, gripping Penny's chin. "I am not your father."

"*Vincent, please.*" Patty gets in between them and holds on to our father's arm.

"You're the only father she's ever known. She didn't know she wasn't yours. Please stop treating her like this just because you have a backup."

Aunt Patty looks over her shoulder at me, her eyes welling with unshed tears.

I stand there, mute, as she glares at me with such animosity I take a physical step back. In all the years I have known her, I have never been on the receiving end of this much vitriol.

"DO NOT CALL MY DAUGHTER A BACKUP!" Santos snarls, his voice echoing as contempt fills his entire body and he starts literally shaking from its gravity.

Then he turns to me, tension making his shoulders coil. He makes up his mind as he stalks over to me, looming over me with his presence and stature. He reaches out, as if to grip my shoulder. Then suddenly, he stills when we hear Noah growl in warning behind me.

My father smirks, his eyes still on me. "Calm down, boy. I wouldn't hurt my own daughter."

I shoot my husband a pleading look.

Please. Stay right there. Don't do anything.

Noah refuses to look at me, blatantly glaring at Santos. His stance is defensive, knees bent like he's poised to jump my father should he even attempt to touch me.

"Noah."

My husband shuts his eyes for a second, reeling himself back in. He sucks in a deep breath before he opens his eyes to meet mine.

His gaze is unsure, jaw still locked tight.

Has my father had control over every person in my life?

I feel the heat of a tear slide down my cheek, scalding my skin in its wake. The pain burns deep inside the cavities of my chest.

There is no way we're leaving here together; I know it. I can feel it.

Noah must see the resolution in my eyes.

He takes a step towards me and I take a step back, shaking my head.

His eyes do a worried dance between mine.

I smile at him, letting him know I got this.

I twist back just in time to see Penny lunge at me from behind Santos.

My eyes shoot behind her over to where Director Villegas stands in shock as he points his gun back and forth between Penny and Aunt Patty.

If he fires his weapon at Patty, he will inevitably hit his boss.

If he fires it at Penny, there's a chance the bullet might graze me.

Aunt Patty's scream echoes throughout the room, much like Santos' did not five minutes ago. Everything happens so fast.

Next thing I know, I'm facedown on the ground with Penny's hands tangled in my hair and what feels like her knee shoved into my back.

Noah

RIA!
I let myself get so caught up in the finality in my wife's eyes, I completely missed Penny inching away from her mom to grab the weapon she had apparently smuggled inside her dress.

Next thing I know, I'm lunging for Santos after Penny strikes him from behind. I underestimated her because just as quickly as I grab hold of her father, she lunges for Ria.

We're at a standoff now.

The room is frozen.

In one corner, I'm standing with Santos in a chokehold while Penny has Ria on the floor, her knee on my wife's back.

Standing opposite me, my old boss still has his gun cocked at Patty while the two useless bodyguards are caught between saving their boss and following orders to protect Ria.

"LET MY WIFE GO."

I can't help but tremble as I eye the pocket pistol Penny dangles in between her fingers while her other hand is wrapped around Ria's hair, holding her face upward.

"I don't take orders from you, Agent."

"P-p-penny…W–w–why are you d-d-doing thi-is?" Ria chokes out, tears streaming down her face. She's gasping, trying to catch her breath as Penny jabs her knee harder into Ria's spine, undoubtedly cutting off circulation.

"You ruined everything, Alessandria!" Penny bares her teeth in anger as she yanks harder on Ria's hair, causing Ria to cry out in surprise.

The sound has Santos jolting awake, after momentarily losing consciousness when Penny clipped him from behind.

"Penelope, what in the world do you think you're doing to your sister?"

Santos' voice is calm, in contrast to the way I'm holding him prisoner.

I suspect he has a weapon on him, but I can't risk letting him go to search for it when there's four rogue weapons that will be trained on me within seconds.

Penny lets out a humorless laugh. "So now that I have a gun on her, we're sisters, but I wasn't even your daughter five minutes ago?"

"Penelope. Stop this madness and let Ria go," Patty interjects.

Patty rises slowly, palms up as she looks over her shoulder at Director Villegas.

Santos shifts suddenly in my arms and in a nanosecond, I have him shoved on the floor in the same way Penny has Ria. The gun he was attempting to remove from his trousers slips out of his hand. I have his arms locked behind his back as the gun lands on the floor, spinning in between Ria's head and his.

I pat him down quickly, looking for more firearms while my eyes are still tracking Penny's movements.

I'll be damned if that gun goes anywhere near my wife.

I find another pistol strapped to Santos' leg.

I aim this one at the back of his head just as his bodyguards finally realize the gravity of the situation. They decide on their target and point their guns at me.

I smirk at them. "Welcome back, boys."

Santos grunts, his face turning red with rage as he continues to stare at Ria.

He's not even looking at Penny, which seems to anger her more.

"What's your plan? Shoot her?" He scoffs, spitting venom with his words. "You won't get out of here alive, and even if you do, you really think I would forgive you if you hurt her?"

Penny's chin wobbles as tears stream down her face. "My whole life, you never gave a shit about me. You were always gone and whenever you were home, you were always keeping tabs on this bitch." She pulls on Ria's hair again. My wife stays silent now, even as her head rears back, and her eyes remain glued to her father across from her.

"You had Mom and I all over town recruiting for your big reveal, like somehow Ria would actually figure out you were trying to get her attention. She was––is, a nobody, Daddy. I'm actually somebody. I lived with her, and she never even knew. How do you expect her to run our empire when she's that stupid? Everything should be m––mine."

Penny screams, "MINE!", and in that moment, she lets go of Ria's hair.

My wife's eyes meet mine, and I see the exact moment she makes her decision.

Within seconds, Ria does the self-defense maneuver I taught her when we were still dating and lived apart. She shoves herself off the floor, causing Penny to fall back, and then she flips, using her leg to trip Penny. In a flash, she gains the upper hand and then she's on Penny, straddling her.

They're wrestling with the gun and my stomach jumps to my throat.

It's slamming itself against my chest, knowing the person it belongs to is mere centimeters away from a loaded gun, but I can't move.

The only chance we have is if I hold on to her father.

I just need to hold out until Ben gets here. Ria needs to get the gun.

A single gunshot echoes deafeningly, its sound bouncing off the walls, followed by Patty's earsplitting scream at the sight of blood pooling on the floor.

My arm goes slack and I'm running to catch Ria from falling even before it makes sense in my head.

Ria

In shock, I fall hard onto the cement floor. The gun hangs between my knees as I stare back at Penny, her eyes as wide as mine. She clutches her shoulder in horror before passing out from the sight of her own blood.

I'm shoved aside by Aunt Patty as she rushes to get to her daughter.

Out of the corner of my eye, I see Director Villegas running past us, heading to Noah, who was intercepted by the bodyguards after he attempted to get to me.

By the time I fully grasp the situation, my husband has successfully disarmed the two bodyguards and knocked them unconscious.

There's a tussle between the two agents now, but my attention veers to my father getting up.

He's heading straight toward me, and that grabs my husband's attention. Noah looks up at me, momentarily distracted, and Villegas takes that opportunity to knock the gun away from Noah. They both leap to their feet before rushing at each other but Villegas is quicker, and he pins Noah to the ground.

Aunt Patty scrambles to her feet and charges straight at me with a scream.

I jump to my feet but she doesn't even get the chance because my father has lunged for her and Aunt Patty is unconscious on the ground next to me within seconds.

I feel like I'm watching a horror movie and somehow got

projected into the screen, helpless to do anything but bear witness to bodies falling all around me while my husband desperately tries to get to me.

My gaze snaps to the monster I supposedly came from.

"Why did you do that?" My voice is shaking as I stare down helplessly at the woman who had pretended to care for me like I was her own. Penny is lying flat on her back about twenty feet away, blood pooling on her sleeve.

My sister?

"Why are you treating your daughter and wife like this?"

I'm backing away from him but he follows each step, ignoring my questions.

For the first time, I see a flicker of emotion in his eyes. It's something akin to concern as his gaze sweeps over me, but that can't be right. This man is vicious. Heartless.

He shot a man in cold blood, right in front of me.

He knocked his wife unconscious with no remorse.

He's letting his daughter bleed on the floor without a second thought.

"She's not my daughter, Alessandria. These two women I entrusted with your life have been lying to me. And that man I shot? He was having an affair with not only Penelope but my wife as well." He stops right in front of me and I hit my back on the wall.

His gaze sweeps me from head to foot. This time he grimaces, his eyes stopping on the patches of dirt and blood on me.

"Not to mention what he tried to pull with you."

My mouth drops open in shock.

"That's right. I know. Patricia filled me in as soon as you called her." He smiles, but it holds no humor as his tone drips with bitterness. "I should have killed him back then, but Penelope begged me to spare him."

I'm shaking my head: my mind is hazy with everything

he's throwing at me. He wants me to understand, speaking with a soft voice, pleading for me to understand the reasons for his actions.

"Alessandria. I had every intention of taking care of you and Penelope, but I found out she had known she wasn't my daughter for years. She, along with Patricia and Colin, had hatched this plan to get rid of you so Penelope would inherit my company."

My heart stops and Gabe's words come back to me in a flash.

Get the girl. Kill the agent.

"Wait. You-you don't mean?"

"Yes, Alessandria. That message the FBI intercepted came from Penelope. I would have never been that sloppy. She took advantage of the fact that I was dealing with the feds seizing one of my bigger shipments—a shipment that was secured by your husband during his work undercover. Penelope had no idea that Noah wasn't with you. She was handling some of our European contacts at the time, and she knew I was indisposed. This was her one chance to get to you without me knowing." He grits his teeth, revisiting a memory that enrages him. "When I was finally able to get in touch with my contact, you were already in witness protection. I was livid, and it didn't take me long to figure out who double crossed me. But I couldn't kill her. Not yet. So I bided my time. I decided then that I wanted all three of them alive to give you that option."

"What option?"

"The option to choose their punishment."

I gasp, my free hand coming up to cover my mouth while the other still grips the gun.

"I would never!"

My father releases a breath, his face full of resignation.

"I can see you are more like your mother than you are me.

Marrying a federal agent has also lent to your ability to only see things in black and white."

His hand grips my chin, tilting it up so he can get a better look.

"You look so much like Chloe. Except for those eyes. Those are mine."

He says it so softly I almost miss it.

I swallow audibly, pressing my lips together to keep myself from flinching.

This was not what I figured would happen when I finally met my father. There is no warmth or fluttery feeling whatsoever. Just sheer terror.

There's intent to murder in his eyes when people don't fall in line.

He's staring at me and suddenly the terror gives way to understanding.

This man is still in love with my mother. He is projecting it onto me thinking I could somehow fill that gaping hole inside him that my mother left. He is taking out his anger at missing a life with Mom out on Patricia. Missing out on being my dad on Penelope.

He will not stop until every person who dares covet me is dead.

And that includes Noah.

His eyebrows shoot up, and he sees right through me.

"If you want to save him so he can get to your son, Ria, you need to come with me."

Tears sting my eyes at the confirmation that he knows about Adrian.

"Don't worry, daughter. I have no use for your son when I have you to run my empire. I will consider sparing your husband's pathetic life in exchange for yours. He can try but there is no way he will get out of here alive. I have more than a dozen men outside of these walls."

He drops his hand, rolling his shoulders back as he turns and marches straight for where Villegas has Noah pinned to the ground. Santos stops to pick up the gun Noah had found on him earlier and aims it straight at Noah.

"This man is not suited for you, daughter. We will find you someone better. Someone who will help you give me a proper heir."

My heart stops, slamming hard against my chest.

My blood rushes to my ears, drowning out sound as my skin flushes, and I know I need to make my decision.

Knowing this is my only chance at getting my husband out of here alive, I raise the gun over my head and fire a single shot.

All three look at me, but it's my husband whose gaze pierces me.

Noah's chin drops, his eyes never wavering from mine as fear invades his every feature.

It's two against one. He thinks he's going to die.

Noah, it's us against the world. Always.

"Let him go."

Santos smirks, snapping his finger at Villegas, who picks Noah off the floor. The director grabs Noah's arms, yanking them behind him. My father stands next to my husband with a giant smile as he shoves the gun against my husband's bloody face.

Noah's eyes turn misty, mouthing the words that have me deciding our fate.

I love you.

I look away, not wanting to waver in my decision. I fight against every beat of my heart that still calls out Noah's name.

I start walking towards them, stopping in between Patty and Penelope's unconscious bodies.

Slowly, I raise the gun. My father laughs darkly.

"What? You're going to shoot me?" He huffs, shaking his head. "You're only prolonging the inevitable, Alessandria. This is my game we're playing here. And I always win."

That's where he's wrong.

I may be my mother's daughter, but I am this man's daughter too.

It's time to call him on his bluff.

He loves me, in his own crazy way.

I raise an eyebrow at him, straightening my posture as I turn the gun until it rests under my chin.

He watches my movements, his brow furrowing, and I can see the internal battle to keep himself calm.

"So what? All this just to have me dead?"

My father's eyes darken with rage, and he sneers. "You don't have the stomach to shoot anyone, let alone yourself, Alessandria."

There's a note of uncertainty in his tone. He's trying to keep himself at bay and control this game he is determined to win.

Too bad I'm playing to win too.

"Watch me." I force myself to grin, despite fear thundering through me at the sight of him holding the gun to Noah's temple. "Dad."

"Drop the gun or I kill the agent."

"No." I make a show of disengaging the safety on the gun and pray this man calls my bluff as I point it at my head. "Let Noah go, or I shoot."

"Ria..."

I have avoided looking at Noah for this exact reason. Once our eyes meet, I see the same pain and terror I feel echoed in his.

I offer him my most reassuring smile, wrenching my gaze from his to look back at the criminal who ruined my life. The one who is now threatening the life of the man who holds my heart.

"LET. MY HUSBAND. GO."

Santos grits his teeth, turning his head slightly to look at Director Villegas, who looks as agitated as he does.

"How do I know he's not going to turn around and hunt me down again?"

I look back at Noah as a single tear rolls down my cheek.

I may regret every moment I spent pushing him away these last few weeks, but I don't regret making this sacrifice.

I keep my gaze locked on Noah's; my smile sad with the knowledge this is goodbye.

My heart shatters on the floor and my chest feels tight and empty in its wake.

I love you.

I lift my free hand, placing it on my chest in the same way he always did when he left to go on assignment.

But this time, I'm the one leaving and I'm not coming home.

My lower lip trembles but I swallow against the pain and whisper the words I know will force his hand.

"Because he promised me."

Noah

My blood runs cold. Nothing in my training or my entirely fucked up life has prepared me for this—the sight of my wife with a gun cocked at her head.

I knew making that promise to her would come back to haunt me. I have to live with this image for the rest of my life.

Vincent Santos might think he knows his daughter, but he doesn't know the first thing about her.

I fight against the urge to curl my hands into fists and body slam Villegas to the ground while I sucker punch Ria's bastard father.

My wife is the fiercest, and most headstrong person I have ever met.

If it comes down to it, she will readily throw her life away if it means saving mine. If it means getting me safely to our son.

I will myself to calm down and reassess the situation for an exit strategy.

I trust Ben. We never made it to the rendezvous with the DEA, they must have some inkling that we were ambushed, given the aftermath of what that did to the I-80. I don't know how long I was unconscious, but it should have been enough time to trace our whereabouts.

In my peripheral, I see the stairs leading up to the office

in the corner. I remember the doors opening up to a parking lot and a body of water.

A plan takes form in my head as I set my jaw, willing Ria to understand what I'm trying to convey without making it obvious.

I will get us out of here.

It will take seconds for me to disarm Santos and take Villegas down, but she needs to keep talking to distract Santos.

Ria just needs to hang on so I can get us out of here.

I have a plan.

Ria

His whole demeanor suddenly changes.

Noah's jaw turns granite, and his entire body goes rigid, like an immovable object. The change is subtle, not enough for the two men flanking him to notice, but I know him well enough.

He is unyielding. My husband has a plan.

My eyes flicker back to my father, who is exchanging looks with my husband's former boss.

It looks like they're planning something too.

Time to up the ante before that happens.

"Did I stutter?" I raise my eyebrow, interrupting their silent conversation.

Both men turn back to me and Santos' face turns red with rage, but he stays silent.

"Maybe it's a foreign concept for you, father. Loving someone?"

Crickets... but he tenses even more.

I smirk, knowing *this* is the foreign concept to him.

Defiance.

"Maybe you're not familiar with that emotion, but the man you're holding at gunpoint? There's absolutely nothing I wouldn't do for him."

Because contrary to my father's belief, I am capable. I will destroy anyone and will absolutely, without a shadow of a doubt, kill for Noah. For Adrian.

"That includes giving up my life if it means saving his."

Piece by piece, his facade starts to crumble as his eyes turn black.

Santos snarls, his grip on the gun tightening, setting me even more on edge, but I stand my ground. I stay impassive, waiting him out.

This man watched me from afar my entire life, and despite his money and connections, he never sought me out. So, the reasons he has in doing so now border on desperation.

He needs me.

He won't risk calling my bluff, and he knows it.

"What's your plan, then? What do you want?"

"Noah gets out--unharmed. You have the means and the power to grant him a clear exit. Get him a helicopter so he can get out safely and faster. Then, I want you to stop following him and setting him up. That goes for your henchmen too. I want him--" I raise an eyebrow, pointedly looking at Villegas with disgust, "--to take the fall for this. I want Noah's name cleared. Then, you will leave my family alone. If you can promise me that, I promise to do as you say."

A sinister smile crosses Santos' face when Villegas starts to stutter. The director's grip loosens on Noah and he stumbles back.

That's when several things happen simultaneously, quicker than I can process.

My father turns the gun on his associate and shoots him dead between the eyes.

Noah rushes to me, quickly disarming me as he engulfs me in his arms.

My father looks over his shoulder at us in surprise, swinging his hand back to shoot Noah.

He fires the gun once, twice, and then a final shot.

My body moves of its own accord. I try to shove Noah off

me, but he clings to me, and I turn instead, the movement causing us to fall backwards with me on top of him.

Searing pain shoots up on my left side, and then my shoulder gets hit.

The room starts spinning. I hear shouting and footsteps as the room starts to go black.

The last thing I see is Noah's blood splattered face looking down at me, and I realize three things at once.

He's running, I'm in his arms, and the blood is mine.

Noah

Only a few hours have passed, but it feels like a whole fucking eternity.

All around me the hospital buzzes as I'm sure it always does.

I bury my face in my hands. Even though they've set me up in an empty room far from the bustle, I can practically feel the anguish and sorrow seeping from every corner of this hospital.

It reeks of death and life, filled with sounds of renewed hope and broken despair.

I've been sitting in the same spot for a while now.

I'm filled with utter fear and fading hope.

Even though I've recounted the events of the last few hours to the new director and fellow agents, I'm still reliving each moment in my head on an endless loop, like a broken TV with no remote to press stop on.

I've already changed and washed off the blood, but I can still feel the warmth and heaviness of it on my skin. I can practically smell the pungent odor that had filled that basement.

Ben and several federal agents, supported by agents from the DEA, had burst into the room just as Santos had fired his gun at Villegas. When Santos saw the agents flanking the room, he turned his gun on me, not counting the lengths Ria would go to save my life.

Even after all was said and done, he still didn't grasp the depth of Ria's parting words.

He still didn't understand our love was enough to die for each other.

Then, his screams of horror filled the room as he realized he might have killed his own daughter, and he charged at us with a gun aimed at my head.

Ben had no choice but to shoot him.

One bullet and he fell to the floor, not unlike the bodies that littered the same floor after losing their lives because of him just moments before.

He died instantly.

From one fucking bullet.

The sound of footsteps stops right outside the door and I shift to high alert.

I lift my head just in time to see Mina walk in, Adrian asleep in her arms and followed

closely by Ben. He has my son's diaper bag slung across his shoulder like this was any other normal day and they were simply babysitting.

And that's when it hits me.

Gabe.

My eyes meet Ben's and he shakes his head.

My gut churns and everything inside me clamors for answers, but Adrian demands my attention. My son stirs, lifting his head and blinking those eyes that are so much like mine. I force a smile and remain silent while I hold out my arms.

Mina places my son on my chest, and I look down at this beautiful boy who is all smiles and spit as he gazes up at me adoringly.

My miracle.

The silver lining in all of this.

Who knows nothing of the danger his parents had been in when his own grandfather tried to kill his father and ended up shooting his mother just mere hours ago.

Who didn't get a chance to get to know his uncle who had done everything to protect him. My best friend who gave up his life to save ours.

I think back on all those nights when Ria and I would talk about starting a family.

We talked about wanting to have a boy, who we hoped looked just like me, and a girl that looked like her.

We wanted to give ourselves the family we never had.

Now, fear invades my being.

I'm unsteady and unsure.

What if Ria doesn't survive?

My thoughts get sidelined when a soft, chubby hand finds its way to my line of sight. Then, my son grabs my nose in the most endearing of ways. His eyes shine and his lips form into another drooling smile.

A sudden, overwhelming surge of love fills me.

"Daaaa-daaa."

That's when I lose it.

"Family of Alessandria Thomas?"

I shoot up from my perch on the empty bed, almost dropping my sleeping son from my chest in my haste.

Mina and Ben are by my side instantly, and I gratefully place Adrian in Mina's outstretched hands.

"I'm her husband," I call out to the bespectacled man walking into the room in green scrubs.

A polite smile flashes over the doctor's face for a moment before he nods at us grimly.

"Do you want the good news first or the bad?"

I grit my teeth in frustration, hating the formality in his tone. "Please just tell me how my wife is, Doctor."

A sigh escapes the man as he removes his glasses.

"Alright. I've been informed of the situation and I understand I'm speaking to federal agents?"

I open my mouth to tell this man to shut up and tell me if my wife is alive or dead when Ben comes to stand beside me, gripping my shoulder. He gives it a reassuring squeeze before he turns to the doctor and addresses him.

"Yes, that is correct. Can you tell us about her condition and when we will be able to see her?"

The man nods, his gaze empathetic.

"Ballistic injuries are incredibly challenging, but she made it here in time. One of the bullets merely grazed her shoulder, and we were able to extract the other bullet lodged just beneath the initial graze. Luckily, it missed any vital organs, and the surgery was successful. The bad news is the bullet hit her shoulder muscles. She suffered from significant blood loss and coded on the table--" He cuts off when I hang on to the railing of the bed, feeling the blood drain from my face.

"Is she alive?" I cry out.

Ben grabs me by the shoulder once again, keeping me steady.

The doctor looks completely unfazed, like he expected that reaction all along.

"--But we were able to secure enough blood for a transfusion. We're getting ready to bring her back soon, but I have to warn you... she is still unconscious and breathing through a tube. We're hoping she regains consciousness quickly. For now we are closely monitoring her recovery. So, uh-- hang tight, Agent Thomas. We're doing everything we can to make sure your wife gets through this."

Everything around me tunnels.

My vision closes in on me.

Adrian gets thrust back in my arms and as always, he centers me, forcing me to regain my bearings and focus on him. He's smiling sleepily at me, his grubby hand curling around my shirt as his eyes slowly blink until they're shut and he falls back into a deep sleep.

Ben firmly grabs hold of my shoulders, urging me to take a seat.

I watch as he crosses the room to where Mina has stood vigil, looking out the window into the corridors, as if that would somehow make the wait go by faster. Ben's hand goes to the small of her back and that should surprise me, but being around them these last few weeks, I had noticed distinct changes in their relationship.

There's something there.

I'm hoping they don't let our jobs get in the way of whatever that is.

Life is too fucking short for that.

I force myself to focus on Adrian.

Ria

I've read books and watched movies where they allude to the fact that when you're unconscious, you're still aware of what goes on around you. Somehow even in a comatose-like state, you can hear your loved ones talking to you and actually understand what they're trying to communicate.

Today, I learned that was a lie.

Or maybe it's true for some people.

But for me, the last thing I remember seeing was Noah's face splattered with blood as he shouted my name and next thing I knew, I was waking up in a hospital bed.

Before I even opened my eyes, I knew.

I spent enough time in them with my mom to recognize the smell and sounds of a hospital.

If I wasn't already reeling from the pain of getting shot multiple times or the trauma of what my father had done, I would be triggered by my surroundings.

I lost my mom in a hospital. I don't want to be here.

I fight against a wave of nausea and attempt to open my eyes.

They're heavy and I struggle, succeeding in opening them just a sliver, until the brightness of the fluorescent lighting has me groaning and I quickly shut them again.

I hear a rush of footsteps and the sound of the light getting turned off before I feel the bed dip next to me. A

IN CASE YOU DIDN'T KNOW

familiar, warm hand presses against my cheek and I once again fight against the weight of my lids to open my eyes.

Noah's handsome, rugged face is the first thing I see.

Concern pinches his brows downward and he's sporting days old stubble.

His eyes are red-rimmed, the sight causing my heart to pinch painfully.

Instantly, I know I've been here for awhile. I peruse the room, scanning every inch of it. There's a bit of light coming into the room from the hallway, allowing me to see that the room is empty except for Noah and myself.

I spy a guest bed but it's immaculate, untouched with a duffel bag sitting on it. An armchair sits beside my bed with a single, rumpled pillow on it. Emotion clogs my throat as I realize Noah has been sitting vigil by my side.

"A-a--" I sputter and cough, unable to muster up a single word to ask where my–our son is. My throat feels gravelly and raw and there's a twinge of pain when I attempt to speak again, making me wince.

Noah places a gentle hand behind my head as he pulls the bed up a little. Then a glass of water materializes in his hand, and he coaxes me to take a few sips before he takes it back, placing it next to me on the table.

He takes hold of my hand, giving it a firm squeeze. He's staring at our joined hands like the weight of the world has been resting on his shoulders as I laid unconscious by his side. I watch silently as Noah shakes his head once, like he's reminding himself to get a grip, and he meets my eyes once again.

A cloud of emotion swims in his sky-blue eyes and he swallows audibly before tentatively grazing a finger across my cheek. He grasps my jaw, kissing me gently on the forehead before resting his against mine.

"I thought I lost you again."

His breath fans my face, lending itself to the vivid memories that are now crashing into me. I'm recalling the past events, from being in that grimy basement to the chase before that to leaving Adrian behind in the cabin.

Noah senses the shift in my body and leans back, his eyes tracing my face and then down my shoulder. I realize I've been holding it stiff.

I dip my chin and scan the rest of my body. My left arm is resting in a sling while my right is covered with bruises. I adjust myself on the bed and I know the rest of my body must be covered with them as well. I shut my eyes once again as tremors of pain shoot up and down my side.

My husband makes a tsk-ing sound before pressing the button to call a nurse for pain meds.

He gently eases me back to rest on the bed, dropping another kiss on my forehead. His fingers brush tendrils off my face just as the nurse comes in, attempting to ask me a few questions while she checks my vitals.

I fight against the gravel in my throat and muster up a few one-word responses. She gets me to drink a few more sips of water before adjusting the flow of the pain meds through my IV. She tells me to rest and lets us know the doctor will be in as soon as possible.

Noah's foot taps impatiently as he waits for her to exit, before focusing those blues on me.

"Let's call our son."

His hand digs into his pocket and he pulls out his phone. He swipes on it, tapping on something before the unmistakable sound of a video call fills the room.

He smiles affectionately at me when I attempt to rise from the bed. Settling himself on the bed next to me, he slings an arm around my waist, carefully avoiding my injured shoulder so I can be more comfortable as I rest on his arm.

A shrill ringing sound echoes in the room followed by

Mina's face on the phone screen. She's all smiles when she sees me.

"Hey! Nice to see you back with us, Ria. You had us spooked there for awhile."

I grimace, resting my cheek on Noah's chest and sliding a glance up at him.

"H-h-how long wa-was I out for?"

"A few days."

His lips graze my temple before tipping his chin down at the phone, urging me to take a look.

I gasp, tears forming in my eyes at the sight of my son. It feels like so long since I last saw him and held him.

My chin trembles as the tears stream down my cheeks.

Beside me, I feel Noah's chest heave under my cheek and I know he's feeling our son's absence as much as I am. His grip tightens on my waist and his fingers start to caress my side in support.

Adrian's sitting on a carpeted floor playing with some blocks, but he starts flailing his arms when he sees me, his pacifier dropping from his mouth. "Ma-maaaa-maa."

Sniffing, I force my voice to remain steady. "He-hey baby, Mama misses you so so so much. I'll see you soon, okay?"

Mina smiles at us from beside Adrian, whose cute hands start covering the camera. "I'll bring him by tomorrow, I promise. Ben might stop by tonight though--he mentioned something earlier when he called."

That has Noah's back stiffening next to me and he fumbles with the phone like he wants to walk out with it, so I don't hear the rest. My hand covers his on my waist in a silent demand to include me.

No matter my physical or emotional state, I deserve to be included in this conversation.

My husband huffs out a breath, but relaxes next to me and directs his attention back to Mina.

"Any new developments?"

Mina comes back into view, and we see her setting Adrian in a jumperoo before she turns to answer the question.

She looks back at us, a thoughtful look crossing her features.

"I'll let Ben fill you in on the details, but I think you should get ready. Now that Ria is awake, they're going to want to talk to her. It's the only way."

The only way?

I open my mouth to ask when I'm interrupted by a short knock on our door.

"That's probably the doctor checking in. We're gonna have to cut this call short. We'll circle back to you once Ben is here."

Mina nods before putting the phone in front of our son and we say goodbye to our baby boy who's sucking on a yellow block, his eyes shining with happiness.

Noah ends the call, and then gets off the bed just as a man in blue scrubs and a lab coat walks in.

"Hey, Doc." Noah greets the man who introduces himself to me before rechecking my vitals and doing the whole song and dance the nurse just did.

I hate hospitals.

I cannot wait to get out of here.

A WEEK. They expect me to stay here for at least a week.

The doctor says something about the bullet missing vital organs but hitting my shoulder muscles so he wants to monitor me some more, just to make sure everything is working as it should. They also need to determine whether or not I will need therapy on my shoulder.

And I think I heard something about a psychiatrist coming to check on my mental health?

Now, Noah and Ben are telling me that the DEA and FBI want to get my statement to confirm my innocence in the crimes my estranged father committed, including my involvement with the injuries Penelope had sustained during our abduction.

Why do I have to prove I was acting out of self defense when I accidentally shot my stepsister?

I was the one who was abducted.

Not to mention the fact that it was my father who shot me.

With a trembling hand, I rub my forehead. A dull throb has taken up residence behind my eyelids and even with all the pain meds they're pumping into me, this ticking pain won't stop.

Ben finally shuts the folder in his hands. He's spent the last hour prepping me for questioning. He's filled me in on everything that happened when Noah and I were abducted and while I was unconscious.

Apparently, Patricia and Villegas have both lawyered up.

Penelope is currently in the same hospital, being treated for gunshot wounds.

Despite Ben's best efforts, he was unable to find any documentation or evidence or even any money trail they could use to charge Penelope.

All they had to go on were statements from Noah and I, witnesses to my father admitting to her involvement. Apparently they had nothing else that would hold up in court.

My father was anything but sloppy. He was thorough, and despite his insistence on not caring about Penelope, the years he spent thinking she was his daughter had softened him up. He protected her even in the afterlife.

Patricia, however, ended up with the most charges against her.

Vincent Santos made sure his wife paid for her betrayal. He made sure she was in everything he was. If he went down, she went down with him. The investigation was merely a formality at this point, and she'll be spending the rest of her life in an orange jumpsuit.

The good news is Ben found deposits made from my father and Aunt Patty's joint offshore accounts to several federal agents and politicians, including Director Villegas.

That traitor will rot in prison.

Bad news is, Penelope is clean as a whistle, so as far the FBI are concerned. Given the lack of evidence, she was as much of a victim in this as I am. She could walk as soon as she gets discharged from the hospital.

And that's where I come in.

The only thing they can pin on her is attempted murder, when she tried to kill me. Both times. Ben was able to trace the initial text message to a number that once belonged to her, Which is

what the feds were waiting on while I was unconscious.

At least there's something—which is doing nothing to settle my nerves.

I'm freaking petrified. It's my word against hers.

But Ben is adamant everything is just protocol and there is no way anyone would take her side instead of mine. They had enough evidence, not to mention the body count my father had left in his crusade to get to me to make a case.

I'm not in any documentation either. My father made sure I am as well protected as Penelope is.

"Ria?"

I focus on Ben and his ramblings, letting him repeat what he said, for his benefit and mine.

"Everything that was in the cabin is being transported

here. It should take about a week at least, given we're doing everything by land." He hands the rest of the folders to Noah who dumps them on the bedside table he's been using as his desk.

Ben shoves his hands in his pockets, giving me a small smile.

"We have agents posted everywhere. In this hospital and more at the safe house where Mina and I are with your son."

He nods his head towards the door. "We should be here bright and early tomorrow. So you should both get some rest. Every person who we found to be linked to your father is currently locked up as we speak. This will be over soon, Ria."

He offers his fist to Noah who bumps it with his before he turns another smile my way.

"I'm going to head out so I can grab some dinner for Mina. We'll see you both tomorrow."

With a wave of his hand, he's out the door, eager to get back to Mina and Adrian.

Once we get out of here, I need to figure out a way to help those two find their way to each other. I owed them my life and more. They protected my family, and now they're taking care of our son so Noah can be here with me.

I'm dragged out of my thoughts when a warm hand covers mine.

Noah's looking at me with concern, his fingers tracing my ringless finger, and I know it's on the tip of his tongue to ask me where we stand.

I did just jump in front of a bullet… bullets for him.

But I can't even begin to wrap my head around any of that and thankfully he doesn't push it.

He simply slides into bed, gathering me in his arms. He's careful not to jostle my injuries. My head burrows in his chest and I can feel every slam of his heart.

My hand slides up his chest, resting above his heart, hoping I can tame the wild beast clamoring to get out. I stroke my thumb against the part of him that belongs to me, trying my best to articulate with my actions just how much I love him.

Noah's hands grasp the back of my neck, his fingers tangling in my hair. He gives it a gentle tug until my chin tilts up.

I meet his troubled eyes that are brimming with a mixture of caution, hope, fear and love.

He kisses the tip of my nose, nuzzling it.

"I thought I lost you," he repeats.

"I thought I lost you," I echo back.

A soft smile tips the corners of his mouth but his eyes remain troubled.

"I'm sorry about your father."

I sigh, leaning back enough so I can look at him fully.

"Honestly? I'm not." I shake my head. "I mean, I am sorry for all the horrible, cruel things he did because of me and what my relation to him has cost you but I'm not sorry he's dead."

My breath hitches as my words struggle to catch up with my thoughts. "I'm sorry that he's not around anymore so he can pay for his crimes, but I'm not sorry he's gone." Then I frown, realizing what I just said. "Does that make me a bad person?"

My husband's eyes trace a path between my eyes, searching for the right words to say.

"No."

He grasps my jaw, his thumb rubbing gently across my cheek.

"No. You have every right to feel that way. What that man did to get to you has nothing to do with you and everything to do with the kind of person he was."

I nod, words escaping me as I hang on to what Noah is telling me.

The trauma my father has left in his wake will live with me for the rest of my life.

"I'm sorry about Gabe."

Pain slashes across Noah's features and he swallows audibly.

I fight to keep the tears at bay, but one escapes. Still grasping my jaw, Noah bends to kiss it away.

"Me too, but it's not your fault, so wipe those thoughts out of that beautiful head of yours."

Sighing, he tucks me deeper into his chest, pulling the covers to my chin.

"I love you, Ria. I can't wait for all of this to be over so we can be a family."

I still, an involuntary response, but he still catches it. He pulls back, his gaze questioning and concerned as he roams my face.

"Ria?"

I guess we're doing this now.

"Noah. I-I'm not ready."

His hands fall off my waist as he turns away from me, rising from the bed.

"I don't understand."

Using my uninjured side, I shoulder my way into a sitting position, my eyes following my husband as he paces the room.

"Noah…"

His name comes out in a rush of breath, barely there, but he hears it.

My husband whirls around, his feet heavy on the vinyl floor as he crosses the room back to me. He stops short of getting on the bed again, his jaw tight and his shoulders straining with the heavy emotions bearing down on him.

"Ria. I thought–"

I can't explain my hesitation or my fear without hurting him, but regardless of how I feel about my husband, I needed to fix myself first. I needed to work on keeping the scary thoughts running through my head at bay. I can feel myself holding on by the barest of threads.

He deserves better, and I have nothing to give him. There's very little of me left.

"Noah… I'm not the same person I was before. The person you married and fell in love with is gone. I've changed, and not for the better. I can feel myself on the edge of falling apart. I don't want to hurt you but I can tell that I am. Every ounce of strength I have, every little bit of self preservation I have left, I need to reserve for Adrian. Our son. Can you understand that?"

Emotion clogs my throat, but in that moment, I feel my hesitation take a backseat as my resolve gets stronger.

This is the right thing to do.

Then why can't I look Noah in the eye?

My heart calls out to him like it's lost without a map.

"It doesn't matter how I wish things could be different. I need to put Adrian first. If that means setting myself aside so I can give him a hundred percent of what little I have left? Then that's what I'll do. It's all I have to give."

Noah's warm hand comes up to grasp my jaw, his thumb tilting my chin up so he can look me in the eyes.

"Then give me fifty." His eyes blaze, turning murky. "Hell, give me ten and I'll provide the rest for us. What do you need from me, Ree? One hundred? Two? A thousand percent? It's yours."

His other hand tangles in my hair. "I'm here now. Let me in. Give us a chance again. Do what you need to do to find yourself and I'll take care of the rest."

His eyes are wild with determination but his pain is

evident. His eyes are rimmed with red, and I can tell he is at the cusp of a mental breakdown.

His love for me is as steadfast as he is—unrelenting.

"I'll be here, holding your hand. I'll take care of you and Adrian. Let me carry the load."

"Noah..."

"I'll give you anything you ask for, Ria, but please do not ask me to give you up."

Without preamble, he lets me go as he climbs back into bed with me, pulling me gently to lay back on his chest. He rubs his cheek against the top of my head but the slight tremble in his hands shows uncertainty and pain.

I hate that I'm hurting him.

I hate that I'm making him feel unwanted.

But this isn't just for Adrian.

This is for Noah too.

I'm *broken*.

Defeated.

Tainted by the crimes of my father.

He deserves more than just scraps.

I love him way too much to not let him go.

"You deserve better than me." I whisper the words against his chest, hoping to ease some of the pain I caused him with my words.

His arms tighten around me, "I deserve you."

Dipping his head, he drops all pretense of restraint and kisses me with the same tenderness and possession that I've always associated with Noah.

"I want you, Ria. Only you."

Noah

Between taking care of Adrian and Ria's recovery, days have turned into weeks in a constant flurry of tests and a barrage of never-ending phone calls.

I spend every free moment I have with my family, and when I'm not, I'm scouring every piece of evidence we have. I want this over and done with in the shortest amount of time possible.

I was taken off the case the second my wife became the subject of it, but I still serve as an advisor, given the time I spent working on the case.

Despite my grumblings, I've been assured several times by not only Ben, but several agents who have done drop-ins that this case is pretty much an open and shut one.

For now, Ben is acting as the lead in lieu of Gabe, with Mina's support.

It would be a slam dunk if we could just find any evidence to pin on Penelope, aside from the two counts of attempted murder we filed against her.

In less than two months, everyone else involved including her aunt and the former Director have been tried and sentenced.

I just have this gut feeling that the death of Vincent Santos doesn't mean Ria isn't safe.

Not yet.

Not until Penelope is behind bars. That woman tried to kill my wife right in front of me.

I shudder involuntarily when I remember everything that happened in that basement. The sight of Ria with a gun will haunt me for the rest of my natural born life.

This shit is messing with my wife. She's been disoriented and closed off.

Aside from that first night when she let me kiss her, she's been otherwise quiet and reserved.

It kills me, knowing she's hurting. It guts me that I can't do anything to help her deal with the pain and trauma. It sucks that she thinks because of all of this, I'm somehow better off without her.

I'm itching to talk to her about us more, but Ria needs time and space to work out her demons and figure out how to deal with the aftermath of what we went through. She needs time to deal with her father's death, his crimes, and her role in it.

Thankfully, we found a therapist she actually likes, but I worry that being cooped up in this apartment is reminding her of the safe house.

She barely looks at me-- not even when it's just the two of us in our room.

The only person she smiles at is Adrian. And sometimes she'll even smile at Mina.

Those two have become closer as they spend more time together in our temporary home.

I look around at the open space of the apartment Gabe's DEA friend put us up in while we awaited Penelope's trial. It's impersonal and bare. There are only two rooms in this place: the master bedroom, which Ria and I occupy with our son, and the guest room, which is being used by Mina. Ben has been relegated to the couch but he doesn't seem to mind.

All his technology is situated in the living room, and he has easy access but now things seem to be different.

In the beginning, Ben had been away a lot while he took part in the take down of the Sotnas cartel, leaving Mina to handle the paperwork aspect of the investigations from here. I helped as much as I could but given my connection to the case, anything I do to assist them could be construed as obstruction of justice.

Thankfully, most of it is behind us and we have one last hurdle to get over.

Ben has now been delegated to assist Mina in protection detail, so he spends most of his time here in the apartment and it's been nothing short of interesting.

The dynamic between the four of us is easy, with little to no tension. But the tension between Mina and Ben? Well… let's just say if I cracked an egg and placed the pan between the two of them, I'd cook the sucker in under a minute.

They think we haven't noticed, but quite a few times we've seen Ben do a hilarious walk of shame out of Mina's bedroom.

In those few moments of camaraderie, Ria looks at me with a hint of amusement coloring her cheeks before she looks away and her mask comes back on.

Once again, we have found ourselves living under the protection of the FBI.

I would laugh at the irony if it didn't remind me constantly of what we've had to go through to get to this point and what we've had to lose to regain even the smallest modicum of freedom.

Sighing from the direction of my wayward thoughts, I push off the dining table. Across the room Ben is shutting off his monitors. Mina is in the bedroom with Ria and Adrian, so we took our time going over a few more things before Penelope's arraignment tomorrow.

Ria will not be required to show up to court until the trial starts and she takes the stand, but both Ben and I will be present tomorrow to ensure everything goes smoothly.

I press a cool hand on the back of my neck, rubbing my aching muscles. Tossing the stack of folders on Ben's desk, I round the couch and ease myself opposite him on the armchair.

"Everything good on your end, Walker?"

Nodding, Ben tips his chair back, his arms crossed behind the back of his neck.

"It's not much, but at least it's something. Homegirl is looking at twenty years minimum."

Not enough time if you ask me, but voluntary manslaughter is all we can charge her with given the lack of evidence.

I grunt in response, pissed that we can't do more.

A few minutes pass as we both stay silent. We're lost in our own worlds. In an attempt to alleviate some of the tension, I get up and grab a few beers from the fridge. Snapping the caps off the bottles, I stride over to him and offer him the cooler one. Ben looks beat. He's carried a lot of the brunt work of this case after Gabe's death and my removal. With Mina also being sidelined to serve as Ria's personal detail, everything has rested on his shoulders. The weight of everything must be getting to him.

"You alright there, man?"

He scoffs, but true to his good nature, he grins and pulls his feet up to rest on the back of the couch. "Yeah, I'm good. The end is near and finally this case is almost over."

He uses the neck of the bottle to point at me. "After this, I'm going on vacation."

A chuckle escapes, despite my better judgment because damn I feel the same type of way.

"I'm good, Noah."

There's an edge to Ria's voice, probably because I've already asked her if she was okay at least five times since I started getting ready.

I'm holding Adrian, who's seconds from dozing off, but my eyes are stuck on my wife who does not look okay, despite her insistence.

Her eyes keep darting to the door and then back to the briefcase I'm bringing to the courthouse and then to our son resting on my chest.

Clutching Adrian closer to my chest, I quietly remove his stuffed duck from his crib and chuck it on the bed. I carefully set him down, patting around to ensure he won't roll over and accidentally suffocate on anything.

With one last graze of my thumb across his soft baby cheek, I sigh in defeat, knowing there isn't much I can do to alleviate the anxiety my wife is feeling.

I know her better than I know myself and right now it's setting her on edge that I have to leave. Adrian was feeling it a bit earlier, clinging to me and getting fussy when I set him down. He cried the whole time I was taking a shower and only calmed down when I picked him back up.

I don't want to leave them either. This will be the first time we're going to be apart since the cabin, but I have to go. This is the last time I'm doing this.

I've already informed the bureau of my decision to leave after the case is wrapped up. I have a few offers floating around that won't involve field work, but I told them I needed time to be with my family before accepting a position.

Rubbing a tired hand down my face, I turn back to my wife.

She's perched on the edge of the bed, her eyes trained on our sleeping son.

"Ria?"

Her eyes flutter shut at the sound of her name and the hairs on the back of my neck stand. Ria pinches her mouth, her hands curling around the comforter on either side of her lap. Her chest rises and falls but her breaths come out unsteady and uneven.

Three steps are all it takes for me to be down on my knees in front of her, my palms on top of her hands as I squeeze them in reassurance.

I'm here.

Ria opens her eyes, and, in that moment, I see it. Not just the fear or the panic but the love she tries to hide from me. She's looking at me in the same way she used to look at me.

I dream about this Ria constantly. Every day, I hope to catch a glimpse of her to tide me over.

"Noah, I'm scared."

I nod.

I know.

"It will all be over soon, baby. Just hang in there a little longer, okay? I'm here. You're not alone in any of this."

I gently remove her hands from the comforter. My hands glide up her arms, careful not to jostle her injured side. It may have healed already but she hasn't quite gotten her strength back.

"What can I do? What do you need?" I look around the room at the cramped space. "Do you want to get a bigger place while we go through this trial? We can do that. We have enough in savings if they can't provide a--"

A startled gasp escapes her, and I stop talking.

"You're giving me a choice?"

I can feel my face scrunch up in confusion, disconcerted by her choice of words.

"Of course. You always have a choice."

Her eyes widen, a tear escaping down her cheeks.

"Talk to me."

I use my thumb to gently wipe away the moisture on her cheek, nervous to hear what she has to say.

"The only time I had a choice in my life was when I decided to be with you, but even that felt like it was out of my control."

She's whispering the words, but she might as well be yelling them at me. Each word punctures, stabbing me with unconscious intent.

There had been several moments during my first year with Ria where I questioned if I was right for her. Knowing the kind of life I lived and the career path I had selected for myself, I had often wished that I had met her sooner so I could have lived differently.

Now that I've heard the words straight from her mouth, I'm left with so much insecurity and resounding guilt.

I let my eyes roam her face before they fall on her hands, now pressed together on her lap.

Still ringless.

I haven't told her yet, but I have her ring. Ben had secured it for me when the FBI sent over the evidence we had been missing. This whole time, it had sat in my former boss' office, along with evidence he had purposely hid to obstruct the investigation.

I've been waiting for the right time to give it to her, but now seeing how this is affecting her, I know she's not ready. I'm still wearing mine around my neck, not wanting to push her about our marriage.

Yes, she lets me hold her and kiss her. But her heart is still locked up in the makeshift prison she built during our time apart.

I don't question whether or not she loves me. I know she does.

Her soul calls out to mine just as much as mine does to her.

She just needs time to work through all the shit in her head. I can wait... but now I'm wondering if I should push a little harder and make more of an effort, so she knows she is the only one for me.

I'm willing to make adjustments to my career so we can function better than we did before.

"Ria. Look at me please?"

Cupping her face, I urge her to turn those gorgeous browns my way. When she finally does, they're welling with tears, her distress palpable.

"I don't want to leave either. The thought of you and Adrian here without me fucking frightens me--" I thread my other hand through her hair, running my fingers through those dark locks that are the stuff of my dreams. "--but I need to be there so I can make sure Penelope stays far away from you. This is what I need to do to protect our family."

I kiss her forehead gently, letting my lips idle over her skin. I bask in her scent, allowing it to consume me like only she can.

Resting my forehead against hers, I move my hand across her cheek to cup the back of her neck.

"I'll be back soon."

She nods against me, her hand coming up to clutch my wrist. I can feel her defenses crumbling and the urge to stay here so we can finally talk about us is strong, but I resist.

One more thing and this will be over.

I need to do this last thing and then I can fight for her. For us.

I rise to my feet, pulling her with me and against my chest.

And because I'm a glutton for punishment, I give in to it. I tip her chin up, my lips crashing down on hers in a kiss that was meant as a see you later that suddenly feels like a goodbye.

Pulling back, I look down at her widened eyes and realize she feels it too.

The uneasiness I felt earlier transforms into something unpleasant. My stomach feels cramped, almost pained, and the weight that settles into my chest becomes even heavier than it was before.

Ria

I woke up with the worst feeling in the pit of my stomach.

I have anxiety and it's normal for me to feel anxious when I wake, especially with what's happening today. But this isn't *just* anxiety--this is something else.

Something almost like a cautionary warning from the universe.

I've had a bad feeling since Noah told me weeks ago that he was going to attend Penelope's arraignment.

I brushed it aside as apprehension, the fear of deviating from our norm.

But today that feeling intensified.

Noah felt it too. The look in his eyes when he walked out the door, his hand halting on the doorknob as he gazed back at me, showed how troubled he is.

But, of course, he had to leave.

My husband is my fiercest protector. His instinct may be to not leave us but his desire to end this once and for all outweighed everything else. He needed to see this to the end.

Besides, we weren't unprotected.

Mina is here. And I know there are agents posted within the vicinity to ensure our safety.

There is no reason for me to be afraid.

My father is dead.

CJ is dead.

Aunt Patricia is in a correctional facility.
Penelope is at the courthouse.
Anyone who could ever hurt me is indisposed.
I am safe.
I think.

∼

BY NOON, the feeling doesn't pass. If anything, it gets worse.

After two hours of complete radio silence from the men, Mina has started pacing the room, checking the doors and windows every so often.

She's on the phone with a fellow agent I'm assuming is outside, given she just ordered a perimeter check.

Another rush of anxiety sweeps through me and I'm filled with the need to prepare for a worst case scenario. I pick up Adrian from his playpen in the living room and head back to my room. I feel Mina's presence behind me and I know she's following me to keep an eye on us. But she stays just outside the room, in the hallway, her phone still pressed to her ear.

I settle my son on the bed with a few toys before heading straight into the closet and grabbing a bag. I start filling it with Adrian's necessities in case we need to get out of here.

Mina watches me out of the corner of her eye, and she gives me a thumbs up, which just spurs me into a further state of panic. My gaze drifts to the lockbox in the corner of the closet where my Glock and Noah's spare service gun are stored. I get down on my knees under the pretense of grabbing some of Adrian's blankets, shifting slightly so all Mina can see is the lower part of my body. I make quick work of opening the safe, grabbing my gun and making sure it's loaded. I check to see if the safety is on before stashing it into a stack of blankets and stuffing that into the bag I just packed.

I toss the bag on the floor next to the bed and sit next to my son, returning the cheeky smile he offers me. I kiss the top of his head, hoping that helps calm the rising panic inside me. I shoot another glance over at Mina who is now staring down at her phone with frustration, her lower lip stuck between her teeth.

I take that moment to jump back to my feet, taking the duffel bag with me and head over to the dresser where I store Adrian's stuff, including his diaper bag. I open the drawers, grabbing a few extra diapers, his milk, and bottles before I spot what I'm looking for.

My gun holster sits at the back end of the drawer.

I hastily look over my shoulder to check if Mina's watching me, but her eyes are still trained on her phone as she attempts to make another phone call. I assume she's calling Ben again. Right now, I won't worry about it. I'm just grateful for her distraction.

I unzip the duffel bag, quickly taking the gun out, stuffing it in the holster, and then, under the pretense of dropping the bags on the floor and zipping them up, I strap in the holster on my ankle. I'm thankful I had the good sense to wear my oversized sweats and chunky sneakers today. My weapon is not visible.

I check the clock, taking note of the time. I make Adrian a bottle, wearing the diaper bag on my back. I grab the bag on the floor and head back to my son. As soon as he sees his bottle, he raises his arms up, asking to be carried. I lift him back into my arms, giggling at his overeager hands. I rock him while he drinks, smiling a little at his eyes drooping as I make my way over to Agent To.

"Mina?"

Pursing her lips, she turns to me but just as she's about to say something, her phone rings. Relief crosses her features when she checks the caller ID.

"Walker! What's going on?"

Mina's relief is short-lived when her eyes widen in alarm. She takes the duffel bag from me, using it to nudge me out the door with Adrian in tow. She stops me just outside her door, her phone still glued to her ear as she listens to Ben. I watch as she grabs her own duffel bag from her bed. That should frighten me if I didn't already know Mina and her incessant need to be prepared.

But when I see a barrel of a gun poking out of the zipper which she hastily stuffs back in, my trepidation comes rushing back.

Adrian gets fussy, sensing my increased state of panic and I hold him close to my chest, shushing him as I wait for Mina to fill me in. I take the bottle from his hands and muster up a smile, clutching him close to my chest as I rock him to sleep.

Mina gestures for me to head towards the living room while she heads straight to Ben's tech. She throws our bags on the couch next to the monitors before doing something on the computers that looks a lot like pulling up data. She yanks a USB drive from the desk drawer and starts transferring data and then she starts grabbing the stacks of paperwork from the desk and shoving them into the shredder underneath the desk.

I feel useless watching her do all this, but I can feel a panic attack coming. My breathing starts coming out in spurts and I struggle to catch my breath. My eyes dart around the room like some unknown enemy is about to jump out from the shadows.

Mina turns to look at me, her eyes narrowed and focused. She's in agent mode, and I know better than to try and have a conversation with her but I'm feeling incredibly out of sorts. I need to do something. Anything.

"How-how can I help?"

She shakes her head, opening her mouth to speak when

her forehead burrows and I hear the distinctly deep rumble of my husband's voice replacing Ben's on the other end.

"Understood."

Nodding her head, she hands me her phone then turns back to finishing her tasks. The loss of the phone speeds up her process-- she's in a hurry.

We're leaving. *Soon*.

"Ria?"

My husband's voice grounds me. My panic is still simmering beneath but somehow, I'm calmer just hearing the sound of his voice, safe in the knowledge that he is okay.

"Ree, I need you to listen to me and not panic, okay? Can you do that?"

I try to extinguish every trace of panic from my voice.

"Yes. What's going on?"

"In about five minutes, several agents will be at the door to escort the three of you to a secure location. Mina will identify them, but do you remember Agent Smith from the DEA?"

"Sarah? I remember her from the hospital."

"I've already told Mina this, but if Sarah isn't at the door, do not leave. Do you hear me?"

"Noah, what's going on?"

He lets out a frustrated grunt and his voice fades away, followed by a car starting. I hear him barking out orders at Ben or whoever he's currently with.

He comes back shortly after, his voice filled with unchecked anger.

"Baby, I'm on my way to where you're being transported but I'm still about an hour away so just follow whatever Agent Smith and To say. They will keep you safe."

My frustration with his nonanswers is climbing to an all time high.

"Noah."

He sighs heavily. I can practically feel the tension seeping through the phone, and I hear a car door slamming followed by tires screeching on the other end.

"Penelope's transport was hijacked. She escaped."

Is the ground tilting? Why is everything spinning?

"Ria. Slow breaths, baby. I'll be with you soon. In the meantime, remember what I said. Agent Smith and her alone-- do not talk to anyone else. Follow her orders and try not to panic."

"Noah..."

"Nothing is going to happen to you. Nothing will happen to Adrian. I promise you." His breath hitches and I know he's clenching his fists, wanting to be here to hold me and protect us. "Trust me, okay?"

My heartbeat increases in tempo, going off in a gallop.

"I do."

"I love you, Ria. You and our son. Just--just please listen to Agent Smith and To until I can get to you."

I lose sight of my heart. It ran off, wanting to be with Noah. Numbness is in its stead, filling me with this gut-wrenching realization.

Penelope isn't going to stop until she gets to me.

Get the girl. Kill the agent.

"Noah..."

"Remember what I promised you." His voice quakes with unrelenting emotion. "Until the ends of the earth, Ria. I'll always catch you. I won't let you fall."

Someone yells for him on the other end and he curses under his breath.

I love you, Noah Thomas.

"I gotta go but I fucking love you, okay? I'll see you soon."

The call ends just as Mina stands in front of me, her task seemingly done. With both bags already back under her arm, she takes a second to look me over as I hand back her phone.

She tucks it in her back pocket, taking the now empty bottle out of my hand as well. She slides it into the side pocket of the diaper bag I'm wearing on my back.

"Hang in there for me, okay? I've got you two."

I swallow down the tears. Mina has become my closest friend.

No. She's more than that--she's become like a sister to me. She's family.

I force a smile, hoping she buys it. Her nose scrunches like she doesn't but we're interrupted by three consecutive knocks on the door followed by someone yelling out, "Agent To."

Mina's back straightens, her whole demeanor changing as she blindly gestures for me to stand behind the pillar. She drops both bags by my foot, making sure Adrian and I are hidden from sight before she makes a move for the door. She keeps her back low, pulling a gun out slowly.

She glances at me quickly, holding a finger to her mouth and making a gesture for me to get down. I squat, gathering Adrian deeper into my arms, grateful he fell asleep at the perfect time.

Mina peers through the peephole before unlatching the lock and opening the door.

"Orders."

"Agent Thomas sent me here. I am to bring his family and Agent To to the designated safe house approximately eight point seven miles south from here."

I recognize the voice. The accent is a dead giveaway. Boston.

It's Agent Smith, just like Noah said.

I breathe a sigh of relief. At least one thing was going right today.

I watch as Mina nods, her expression never wavering as her eyes scan the visitors. Slight hesitation mars her features as she looks over at me. I frown but she gives me a slight shake of her head.

She turns back to our visitors and holds up a hand. "Stay here. No one is to step foot inside this apartment until I can secure Agent Thomas' family. Understood?"

Mina's brow raises, waiting for their acknowledgement while she secures her weapon back in its holster. She must get it because she starts walking backwards toward me, her fingers stretching around her weapon just in case of an ambush.

As soon as she's standing next to me, she hunches down to grab the bags but pauses so she can whisper to me.

"I don't recognize one of them so just make sure to stick to me at all times, okay?"

I give her a stiff nod, pretending to adjust Adrian in my arms.

She knows what she's doing.

I trust her.

I follow her out the door and all the other agents fall back as Agent Smith steps up. She gives me a reassuring smile when something in my face must allude to my distress.

"Mrs. Thomas. Twenty minutes. Do you think you can hang on for that long?"

I nod at her. I'm still unsure of the proper etiquette for these types of situations I keep finding myself in.

All I can think about is how Noah isn't here and Adrian is going out into the open where Penelope could be anywhere, hell bent on killing me.

We're shuffling into the elevator when I feel it. A note being shoved in my pocket.

On our way down the hall, Mina made sure she was always behind me, Agent Smith leading the way. But when we entered the elevator, both agents had secured themselves on either side of me. I didn't bother looking at the other agents, Noah's words echoing in my head. But the note was passed on my right side as I entered the elevator, meaning the person who passed it was now in front of me on my left.

I don't dare make it obvious with Adrian here. The last thing I want is some rogue agent training a weapon on me while I'm holding my son.

I let my eyes drift slowly and take note of the agent's appearance.

Medium height.

He looked about my age with blonde hair clipped on the sides.

I look for anything specific that can identify him later on should I lose sight of him, and that's when I see it.

He has a tattoo on his neck. The same one CJ and my father were sporting on their arms.

Is that the cartel's tag?

The elevator dings and Mina clutches my elbow, hustling me out.

We stop a few feet from the door with Agent Smith positioning herself in front of me. Her hand goes to the earpiece she's wearing.

"Location?"

She nods at the other agents, pointing to the doors as they exit first to do a periphery check. Then a black Ford Expedition rolls in and an agent steps out, holding the door open.

Mina propels me forward as Agent Smith brings up the rear. All the agents have their weapons drawn, their eyes scanning the area.

I settle into the backseat of the car with Mina right beside me. There's an agent crouched down with his weapon drawn right behind us. Agent Smith gets into the passenger seat of the car, then speaks into her earpiece.

"We've secured Nala and the cub. We can proceed."

Startled, I meet Mina's eyes and she gives me a small smile. "Noah."

The Lion King is Noah's favorite movie.

I just know he was banking on me hearing them, maybe even asking Agent Smith to make sure I heard them refer to me that way. He wanted me to feel safe even without his presence.

Unfortunately, hearing his fellow agent calling me Nala only gives me a shallow sense of security once I remember the slip of paper in my pocket.

Penelope.

She still has eyes and ears in the bureau.

I wait until we've started moving before I discreetly take the paper out.

There's nowhere you can hide where I won't find you.

If you don't want to see your family get hurt, you'll do as I say.

Or watch as I kill them right before I kill you.

After three blocks, your car will be blocked for approximately fifteen seconds.

Use that time to escape.

There will be a gray suburban on the left side of the street.

Get in.

Let's finish this.
   -P

. . .

IN CASE YOU DIDN'T KNOW

I STILL. My chest pinches and my vision spirals. I shut my eyes against the tidal wave of emotions threatening to push me further down an oblivion of anxiety and fear.

As long as Penelope is out there, my family will never be safe.

She *will* find me.

She already did.

I open my eyes to glance down at Adrian sleeping peacefully on my chest. He's grown even more in the past few months.

I'm going to miss so much of his life.

The realization that this may very well be the last time I see him or hold him has me choking up. My eyes burn from the unshed tears but I will them away.

I need to stay strong.

This is for Adrian. For Noah.

Their safety--their *lives* mean more to me than anything in this world.

I pull my son closer to me, breathing in the scent that's solely his.

I whisper words of love to him, hoping he grows up to be as brave, loving, patient and dedicated as his daddy is. I know he's still very young, but I hope he remembers me.

I hope he grows up knowing just how much I loved him and that he takes my love with him wherever he goes. I hope he never feels lonely or sad or alone in this world.

I trace his features, memorizing every detail and storing it so I can hold on to it when I need it.

I'm once again struck by how much he looks like his daddy.

Cerulean eyes, cherry lips, and chestnut hair.

Noah.

I hope my husband understands that I love him beyond comprehension.

That loving him felt a lot like walking into a house and suddenly knowing you're home.

Falling for him wasn't falling at all.

It was coming home. *He is home.*

But it wasn't safe anymore-- not for him and not for Adrian.

Noah can't be my safety net if his life would constantly be on the line.

I hope he understands that because I love him, I have to go.

There's absolutely *nothing* I wouldn't do for him including betraying him by leaving now.

I have to go.

I slip the note under Adrian's sleeve, hoping he stays asleep.

I'm grateful that Mina stayed back to be with me today. There is no one in this world besides Noah that I trust with Adrian.

We're at the second block already and I pray the car's child lock isn't on so I can make my escape.

We stop at the light, and I muster up every single scrap of strength I have to nudge Mina. She turns back to me, nodding her head at the agent behind me to keep an eye out the windows.

I paste on the best apologetic smile I can fake and hand her my son.

The car starts moving again, we're about to pull up to the light on the third block.

"Can you hold him for a sec? I think I pulled something when we hightailed it into the car. Just need to stretch for a few then I can take him back."

There's a furrow between her eyebrows, her worry evident on her face but she humors me, taking Adrian.

I make a show of massaging my arms and elbows.

The car comes to a stop and Agent Smith curses.

Both Mina and the other agent look over to see what the commotion is. That's when I see a man in a wheelchair tipped over in the middle of the crosswalk.

"Mina..."

Her gaze snaps to me and I see the second it clicks as she shakes her head at me.

"Tell Noah I'm sorry. Tell him I love him."

My door flies open at that exact same time and the agent who handed me the note pulls me from the car. I don't resist as Agent Smith shouts for the other agent to grab me.

"RIA!"

Mina attempts to reach out but with Adrian in her arms, she fails to grab me and I land on the asphalt. I see the other agent scrambling to get across the backseat to get to me.

I meet Mina's eyes with my tear-filled ones as I'm dragged to the gray suburban that's waiting.

The door flies open, and he shoves me in.

I hear a scuffle just outside the car before it peels off.

I shut my eyes as I'm bound and gagged.

I finally let the tears fall.

Please forgive me Noah.

Noah

We managed to shave off ten minutes of travel time with the police escort but we're still thirty minutes out.

I wanted to drive but both Lieutenant Keaton and Agent Walker forced me into the backseat like a suspect. Garrett Keaton is a friend of mine from Washington, where I worked as a CSI and he's been helping us gather evidence on Penelope. He flew in today with some local intel to help present to the court but then shit went down.

The second we heard about her escape, we hauled ass, not bothering to wait for direction from our superiors. Ben made transport arrangements over the phone while Garrett talked me out of shooting everyone on sight who got in my way.

Ben tossed Garrett the keys to drive while he finished setting up the safe house we were sending Ria and Adrian to.

I clench my jaw to stop another row of expletives from falling out of my mouth. This is no one's fault but my own, because like a rookie, I ignored my instincts.

I fucking knew it.

I knew in my gut this morning-- something felt off.

The universe was telling me not to leave my family, but I still did.

Right before we got in the car, we got word that Judge

Nolan was found dead in his quarters, right before Penelope's transport got hijacked and she escaped.

It looked like Penelope learned a few tricks from her father, and she definitely had some common connections. She wasn't as useless as he made her out to be.

Ben cracks his neck, his eyes fixed on the side mirror. Luckily, he was also able to secure backup for us in case we got ambushed, and they were following us to the new safe house.

His phone starts ringing, and with an eye still trained on our tail, he answers it absent mindedly.

Then he stills, almost comically turning back to look at me with wide eyes, his mouth agape.

A tremor shoots up my back.

I know what he's going to say before he even says it.

My heart speeds up violently against my chest, sweat beading around my forehead and neck.

I scream out her name before Ben can even speak.

"Ria!"

Ria

I hear her before I see her.

The unmistakable sound of her laughter.

Back when I lived with her, it grated on my nerves because it usually meant she was either throwing another rager or bringing home strays. Both usually meaning drugs and alcohol.

It's no secret we never got along but the antagonism was always one sided. I never hated her. In fact, I didn't feel anything but sadness when it came to her. I wanted us to be friends, given our mothers were close and friendships for me were hard. I craved that connection with her and when it was clear I would never get it from her, I did my best to stay away. But it never worked. She would find a way to antagonize me like it was her job.

She would purposely have parties when she knew I worked or had class early the next day.

Every single time I headed out the door for work or school, she would wave her fingers at me, smirking in a way that clearly said she knew what she was doing.

The kitchen was always trashed and emptied out by her friends so after a while, I knew I had to make daily trips to the grocery store by the café if I ever wanted to eat.

Things got a little better when I moved into the master bedroom and I could soundproof the room. Now knowing what I do about Penelope and how deep her hatred for me really went, I can say for certain that she had always been out to get me. The only thing stopping her was her father's wrath but once he was gone, there was no one to protect me and stop her from doing what she's always wanted: to get rid of me.

The gag cloth and wrap around my eyes are suddenly, forcibly removed. I fall on my ass as my hair tie gets broken in the process. My hair fans around me, obscuring my view of her until someone uses it to pull me up. I swallow down the sting and focus on the fact that at least they didn't pull my weak shoulder. I don't want to give Penelope more ammunition against me.

My hands are tied in front of me and while getting yanked to my feet, I realize they never took my gun.

They never thought to frisk me because Penelope doesn't know this version of me. The one married to a Federal Agent who made sure she knew how to fire a gun and defend herself.

A burst of adrenaline shoots through me, and I feel myself smirking as my eyes finally meet my sister's.

I let my eyes drift over her, taking in the subtle changes since I last saw her two months ago.

She's thinner, her ivory skin pale contrasting her brunette hair that's pulled up. The dark circles around her eyes and her hollowed out cheeks are evidence of the change in her lifestyle.

I look around the room, noticing there are only two other men in here: one standing next to her and one behind me.

From the looks of it, she didn't have enough time to plan any of this out.

We're in what looks like a house with no one living in it. Only a table and a handful of chairs occupy the room we're in and looking past my charming sister, I can see a kitchen bare of any appliances, not even a fridge or microwave in sight. There's a hallway beyond the kitchen but I only spot two doors.

A sheet has been draped across the sliding doors to my right, leading out to a backyard but the sheet they repurposed as a curtain is blocking me from seeing anything past the shrubs on the side.

I have no idea if there are neighbors that can hear me scream for help.

A chair scrapes back, turning my attention back to my captor.

Penelope bares her teeth at me, almost growling in annoyance, which only makes me smile wider.

The entire time I've known her she's been cruel to me and I'm not going to do her any favors by making this easier for her.

"What the fuck are you smiling at me for?"

I shrug, my hair sliding across my cheek.

"I'm simply happy for you." I raise my bound hands. "You got what you wanted."

She raises an eyebrow at me, crossing her feet. She's sitting on a wooden chair, a gun resting on the table next to her, its barrel pointed straight at me. Her fingers dance around it, like she wants to make a point that she's going to shoot me.

The thought of her little production makes me roll my eyes which spurs Penelope to jump to her feet and head straight to me.

Her henchman still has his hand wrapped around my hair but at her approach, he lets go and I hear him take a step back.

Penelope is a few inches taller than me, so I lift my chin up to look at her as she comes to a stop in front of me. Her hand comes out, wrapping around my throat and she squeezes. *Hard*.

I curl my fingers inward, letting the bite of nails cutting my palm distract from her chokehold.

"I'm going to kill you."

Her voice drips with disdain, her hatred for me palpable.

I simply return her glare, choosing not to speak so as not to give her the satisfaction.

She abruptly lets go, making me falter on my feet for a second as I gasp for air. She laughs again but this time in a way I can only describe as nasty.

Her mouth tilts up, her eyes light up and she looks almost giddy at my discomfort.

"Got nothing to say now, Alessandria?"

"What do you want me to say? You won, Penelope. Are you happy now?"

She scoffs then, her eyes turning wild with fury.

"Won!?"

I remain silent, my eyes never leaving hers.

Penelope is coming undone. Anything I say will only further set her off.

Her ponytail flings as she spins on her feet, stalking over to where she left her gun. Picking it up, she points it at me.

"You bitch!"

Anger rises in me, fury unleashed like I've never felt before. and I feel my whole body heat up.

"I'm the bitch, Penny? You made my life a living hell, hunted me down years later, ordered my husband to be killed, and forced me to go into hiding because you tried to kill me. And now I'm here again! For what? What did I ever do to you besides share the DNA of your father?"

Screeching, her arms flail as she unleashes all her anger towards me. Her words are as venomous as she is.

"My father? That man loved you more than he ever loved me, even when he thought I was his. He was hellbent on you taking over for him..." She laughs without humor, the sound hollow as she grits her teeth at the memory. "Like you could ever. You've always been weak, Ria. Too nice. Too fucking trusting." She spits out that last word like it grossed her out. "Bland."

Penelope clenches her free hand into a fist, smacking it against a pillar as she stalks back to me with a vengeance.

"You took everything from me and now I'm going to make you pay for what you did."

A sense of calm rushes through me. I feel a gentle gust of wind followed by the smell of coconut and citrus.

Mom.

Somehow, I know she's here with me, protecting me and lending me strength.

So I do what she's always done-- what she's always taught me.

I attempt the one thing I know will throw Penelope off-kilter.

"Tell me, Penny. What exactly is it that you think I took from you? What have I done personally to you that's made you so mad?"

I try to understand her.

Sighing, I give her another once over. Seeing for the first time exactly what my father has done to her by denying her the one thing she craves most in the world.

Love.

She stops right in front of me, one hand still clutching the gun while the other is fisted, her knuckles red and bruised from when she punched the wall. She's watching me carefully now, her face turning almost curious.

"Penny, I'm sorry he brainwashed you into thinking I'm the enemy. I've never in my life thought ill of you or wanted anything from you other than friendship."

Penelope's eyes darken. She raises an eyebrow and then she extends her free hand, a pocket knife materializing from behind me. Her henchman hands it to her. She keeps her eyes locked on mine as she cuts the zip ties binding my hands together.

I look down at my unbound hands, stretching the numbness and soreness away as I rub my wrists from the cuts the zip ties had caused.

I gasp when she uses the tip of the knife to tilt my chin up, nicking my skin as she forces me to meet her gaze. Then she gestures to the man behind me.

"Zane."

Rough hands wrap around my arms and before I can even blink, he's twisted my arms behind me and I cry out in pain. My shoulder that's still healing throbs like a motherfucker and blood starts dripping down from my chin to my chest.

A satisfied grin pulls Penelope's mouth.

"You want to know what you did to me, Ria?"

I don't answer her, my eyes straining against the pain.

"You existed."

She drops my chin, chucking the knife carelessly against the wall like all sanity has left her body.

"You act like you're above all of this." She barks out a short laugh. "But money is everything, Ria. It changes everything." She takes her time looking me over, her eyes lighting up as it lingers on the blood pooling on my chest. "It can even kill your incessant need to be this good person."

"Penny." Her name comes out in a rush of breath. I ignore the pain as best I can because though I feel like she might be a lost cause, I still want her to know I am not her enemy.

"I'll keep repeating it until it gets through to your head. I don't want any of it and I don't think I'm

above it all. If he––our father–– had just come to me instead of doing all this... I would have politely declined." I jerk my head up, ignoring the sting of the knife cut and the almost numbing pain shooting up my shoulder and back. "You were always meant for bigger things than me. I've only ever wanted a simple life. I would have never taken what you rightfully deserved-- what was always yours."

Her mouth drops open in surprise before she shakes her head, refusing to believe me or my words. She keeps shaking it until the rest of her starts to shake too.

Repressed pain and the aftermath of Vincent Santos' rejection fuels the anger she has for me. Like a movie, her emotions play out on her face as she looks away and starts to pace.

Then the fury comes back, and she whirls back around, once again pointing her gun at me.

"He left me nothing. Did you know that?"

I strain to keep my eyes open, but I keep them locked on hers. I start to feel the weight get heavier in my stomach and the daunting realization of this truly being the end of my life prompts me to face her head on.

She's stuck in her head. She's so far gone, lost in the memories and years of emotional abuse and manipulation she endured. The look on her face turns crazed and without warning, Penelope screams. The action is so sudden that Zane's hold on me loosens a bit in surprise and he shifts, not knowing what to do. The other man who's been standing against the wall behind Penny turns away, looking almost afraid. It's clear these men know her and the capabilities of her anger.

Fear starts creeping up my spine. Though I've known her for a long time, I don't know *what* she's capable of.

"What are you talking about?" I have to force the words out.

She sneers at me, her gait unsteady. "I didn't inherit a single thing. Everything in the company was left to his relatives in the Philippines. I worked hard. Expanding our clientele and because of me, we cornered the market in Europe. And what do I get to show for it? Jail time with no inheritance? Because of you?"

"Do you hear yourself Penelope? I just found out about him and the truth of who you all really are. I spent my whole life not knowing about all of this. You and your family threaten my life, my family's life and now you're paying for your sins and somehow it's my fault?"

"BECAUSE IT IS!"

I snort. I don't want to rile her any further but her persistent need to blame me for her actions and the actions of *her* father is pissing me off.

"Except it's not and I suspect you know that because you're the one with a gun aimed at me, Penny. If this is solely about revenge, what exactly do you gain from killing me besides knowing you killed the object of your father's obsession? Are you really angry at me or are you getting back––"

My voice dies out when another scream pierces through the air and this time she charges at me with purpose. She disengages the safety on her gun.

I have minutes if not seconds left of my life.

She's going to kill me.

I shut my eyes and think about the two people I love most in the world.

Noah.

Adrian.

How I wish I could be with them right now, in the safety of my husband's arms holding our son. Noah and I may not have had the best luck in life, but we managed to come out on the other end. If fate happens to grant me another chance to be with them, I won't focus on the negative or take anything for granted again. Bearing witness to what their money has done to my father, to Penelope, to Aunt Patricia...

I know for certain that I am the fortunate one in all this. I won the life lottery when I fell in love with Noah.

I've lived a full life with no regrets because at the end of it, I was privileged enough to be his wife and have Adrian, the beautiful fulfillment of that love.

I hang on to that.

A crisp sound slashes through the air, like tapping on a table but intensely forceful.

The hands that were holding me captive suddenly fall away and I feel Zane fall before I hear it. His legs bump mine and I drop forward onto the floor. I manage to open my eyes in time to catch my descent, enabling me to use my good shoulder to take the brunt of it.

My eyes snap up at Penelope, who is standing above me, her hand still aimed upward. She gives me the briefest of glances before she turns her gun towards the other man, who is now gaping at her in shock.

Like father, like daughter.

Knowing I have a few seconds before she decides it's my turn, I grab my Glock still stored in the holster around my leg and scramble off the floor.

By the time she shoots him and turns back to me, I'm safely out of reach, on my feet and armed.

Penelope's widened eyes meet mine, her gaze falling on the gun I'm holding and for a split second, the shock gives way to a twinge of fear. She's completely unhinged.

"How--Where?"

My shoulder burns and my back aches from being manhandled. There's blood pooling on my chest and all over my neck. I'm sore from being dragged through the street and shoved around in a van but for the first time today, I smile my first real smile.

"There's one thing you forgot about me and another you don't know."

Penelope scowls, her teeth bared, on par with the paleness of her skin.

"And what is that?"

I take note of the knife she so carelessly tossed earlier that's resting just a few feet away, right next to Zane's head.

"I never give up." I make a show of disengaging my own gun. "And I'm the wife of one of the most decorated agents in the FBI. I'm no longer the helpless girl you used to know."

"Congratulations, Alessandria. What are you going to do? Shoot me?"

Penelope laughs, her eyes crinkling in amusement.

"Kill or be killed."

Her laughter dies replaced with another scowl, more menacing than the last.

"Then let's fucking do this then."

Noah

I slam the door open, not bothering to make eye contact with Agent Smith. My attention is honed in on the blond currently handcuffed to the table.

"Agent Thomas!" Sarah tries to get in between me and the man who impersonated a field agent and abducted my wife, but I brush past her.

"Where is she!?" Fisting his collar, I yank him to his feet and shove him against the wall. *"Where's my wife?"*

"I don't know man!"

I growl, shoving him harder, the legs of the table scraping like nails on a chalkboard across the floor as it's dragged along. I hoist him further up at the wall. My fingers close in on his throat and I squeeze.

"You have five seconds to tell us where she is or so help me, I will choke the living shit out of you and take great pleasure in it."

He stutters, his breath coming out in wet gasps. "Go ahead and kill me, but you'll never find her!"

"Don't test me."

Two pairs of hands come around me, restraining me and making me lose my grip. Our suspect falls hard on his ass, slamming his head hard on the wall on his way down.

Agent Smith lets out a string of curses before shoving me

out the door. The two officers who had pulled me back attend to the suspect now passed out on the floor.

His arms flailing as he regains consciousness is the last thing I see before Sarah jerks the door closed behind her. "What. The. Fuck. Was. That. Agent?"

"He knows where she is!"

"We all know that, Noah. But we do not manhandle suspects, ever. This is why I told you to stick with Walker. You're too damn close to this case. You're going to get the book thrown at you for misconduct!"

Thrusting my fingers in my hair, I start pacing the hallway.

"What the fuck do you expect me to do? Twiddle my thumbs waiting for Ben to trace the car they took her in? She could be dead by then!"

I'm filled with unchecked rage, like an explosive device about to go off at the slightest provocation. I'm terrified. Over an hour has passed since my wife's been taken, And so much can happen in that time. They could have taken her out of state by now, or worse… killed her.

"Then go sit with your son. Be with your family, Noah. Let us handle this."

"I'm not going to sit in your office like a damn civilian, Sarah." I glare at her, my words laced with sarcasm. "Do you really expect me to wait around after you all did such a fine job protecting her?"

Sighing, she shakes her head in disbelief.

I know it's not her fault. She came as a favor to me and had no idea the team backing her up had a fake in it. There was no time for her to verify their credentials when she rushed at my request.

"This is not the time to be pointing fingers, Agent."

I grunt in frustration, my back thudding against the wall as I slump down on it. I bury my face in my hands, desperation and agonizing fear seeping through every atom in my body.

Ria.

"Noah--" She gets cut off by the sound of pounding footsteps echoing through the halls.

I look up to find Ben and Garrett rounding the corner into the hallway in a hurry.

"We have an address! Let's go!"

I don't need to be told twice. I jump to my feet and sprint out the door, Agent Smith on our tail.

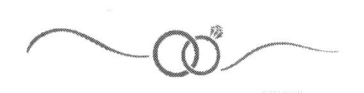

Ria

"Is that all you got?"

Using my elbows as leverage, I spit out blood from Penelope's sucker punch.

After she threw the gauntlet earlier, proclaiming our need to finish this one-sided vendetta, I taunted her about hiding behind guns and money, knowing I would have a better chance at getting out of here if we fought hand to hand as opposed to shooting bullets.

Like a rabbit to a carrot, she took the bait. She throws her gun behind her, and we have a scuffle not unlike the one we had in the basement but this time with no weapons and no one to run interference.

One second, she gets the upper hand and the next, I'm on top of her, jabbing her with my fists. I channel every bit of training I've gotten from Noah and self-defense classes into making it an even match.

I don't know how long we've been at this but at some point, we both jump to our feet and charge at one another. I manage to evade her first few punches, landing blows on her stomach and head but then she fakes a punch and successfully lands a hard one straight for my nose, causing me to hurl backwards. I manage to extend a foot to trip her and she falls, landing on her shoulder with a yelp.

My fucking body is screaming but I suspect the adrenaline rush is numbing most of the pain.

My focus is getting out of here and back to my family by all means necessary.

I stumble to my feet, as the room spins slightly, but I keep my eyes trained on Penelope. She's not as quick as I am this time and she starts to struggle.

I scan her from head to toe and that's when I notice it. She landed on the knife she had chucked earlier, and it's now jammed into one of her legs.

She screams in pain, clutching both her shoulder and leg.

My eyes inspect the rest of the room, taking note of every single weapon I see. With one hand on my injured shoulder, I hop and grab every discarded gun, taking out the magazines and scattering the bullets as quickly as I can.

Finally, I pick up my gun from where I dropped it after she jumped me. I clasp it with a shaky hand and point it at Penelope. She's gritting her teeth as she writhes in agony on the floor, her face pale and defeated.

"It's over, Penny."

She shakes her head, closing her eyes.

"I hate you, Alessandria."

"I know."

"I hate him more."

"Me too."

"All-all I wanted was for him to love me and see-see me."

Penelope chokes out the last word before falling into a fit of tears.

Silent tears stream down my face in unison with hers, hurting for her and for me. Hurting for the relationship we could have had, if only our father had understood what love was. How different could our lives have been?

"I know…"

The sudden sound of tires screeching and car doors slamming has me gripping the gun tighter. Then comes the distinct sound of a familiar voice yelling "FBI!" before the front door crashes open and Ben's around the corner, followed by Agent Smith and…

Noah.

At the sight of my husband, I fall to the floor in relief and like always, he's there catching me before I hit the ground. The gun falls just between my knees. My shoulders hunch over and instantly the adrenaline melts away and I feel *everything.*

Noah

She's the first thing I see. The only thing.

I run to her as she starts to falter, and I catch her before she falls. I drop down to my knees with her in my arms, my chest tightening at the sight of her. Pain slashes through me, warring with the pride I have for this damn woman.

My girl.

My wife.

Ria put up a fight.

I gently tip her chin up, and those beautiful eyes brimming with tears meet mine. I grimace, my heart aching for what she must have gone through. Her clothes are tattered and torn from what must have been an intense battle to stay alive. There's blood everywhere. I gently remove the gun from her lap, tossing it behind me. I'm aching to take her further into my arms but I'm so afraid to hurt her even more.

"Noah--"

She collapses, burying her face on my chest, her shoulders shaking with relief and pain. She repeats my name over and over in hoarse sobs, dragging in air in sharp gasps.

"Shhh..." I rest my cheek on the top of her head, my hand cupping the nape of her neck.

Beside me I can hear Sarah read Penelope her rights as

medics check her. Garrett and the other agents are gathering evidence and taking pictures of the crime scene. Ben is standing in the middle of the room, his hand on his forehead as he glances around. He has his phone pressed to his ear and I know he's calling Mina to update her.

My eyes wander around the room before I shut them, knowing whatever happened in this room will haunt my wife for a long time.

"We're just going to grab the equipment we left at the scene then we'll head to the hospital. Hang in there, Mrs. Thomas."

I wait for the medic to climb out of the ambulance, returning his smile as he passes me to go back into the crime scene to pack up before turning to my wife laying on the stretcher.

I watch as she discards the wipes she used to clean up her face in the trash. She insisted on cleaning herself up because she didn't want to scare Adrian with all the blood. Mina is meeting us at the hospital with our son as neither Ria nor I want to miss another moment with him.

"Hi." She whispers, extending her hand to me.

I take it, pressing a kiss on her knuckles and nuzzling it with my cheek.

"Hey."

"We have to stop meeting like this."

I reach over with my other hand, grazing my fingers on her cheek.

"This is the last time, I promise."

She watches me, her eyes bursting with so much emotion. I stare back, not wanting to break the connection.

"Noah?"

I hum in response, still cuddling her hand. Her smile is

slow but when it comes, it's brighter than all the stars in the damn sky. Like a constellation, the sight of it takes my breath away.

"I love you."

My heart thuds against my chest. I slide my palm downward so our fingers intertwine and I lean into her hand.

She finally said it. *She loves me.*

I carried no doubts but damn it feels good to hear it again.

"I love you too."

My fingers dance from her cheek to the back of her neck as I reposition myself to sit beside her on the stretcher. My eyes dance around her face until she tilts her head, and her eyes start to linger on my lips.

With a grin, I lean in.

I nip the sides of her mouth first, teasing her until she cups the back of my head with her free hand pulling me closer to her. I give in, rewarding her--us, with a slow, languid kiss that quickly deepens, making us both groan in tandem until a throat clears from behind me and the doors to the ambulance cabin shuts.

She giggles, moving her hand that's tangled in my hair to press against my chest. She taps me on the chest, breaking the kiss. She peers up at me, nuzzling her nose on mine.

"Can we go home now please?"

For the first time since I found that note in our kitchen almost two years ago, the weight pressing against my chest disappears as love, hope and an astounding amount of gratitude take its place.

"I can't think of a single thing I want more."

She kisses me softly, her lips pressing into a smile against mine.

"Thank you for catching me."

I rest my forehead on hers.

"Until the ends of the earth Ria, I'll always be there to catch you."

Epilogue

Ria

I sigh in contentment. It's been a while since I fully felt at peace but here in Noah's arms, with Adrian safe and sound, back here in the house we built, I feel it. I'm happy.

Noah rests his chin on my shoulder, tucking my back closer to his chest as his hands fully wrap themselves around my waist.

"What are you thinking about?" His breath on my neck, as he places a soft kiss there, causes goosebumps to rise and my heart to flutter in response.

I turn my head to look at him, resting my forehead against his.

"That I'm finally where I want to be."

He rubs my nose with his and my eyes flutter close. His lips graze mine.

"Where's that?"

I turn in his arms, leaning far enough that my back is now resting against the balcony.

A playful smirk ghosts his lips as he lifts me to sit on the ledge. I rest a hand on top of his chest, feeling his heartbeat quicken against my palm.

My favorite sound in the entire world is his heartbeat.

It tells me he's alive. It tells me he's still mine.

"With you."

"Yeah?"

My breath quickens when he lowers his head, giving me a kiss filled with a lifetime of promises. When he finally breaks it, we're both panting and flushed. I grip the back of his neck to bring him back to me when he shakes his head, his eyes blazing with heat.

"Do you know where my favorite place in the world is?"

I shake my head in response, but my stomach flip flops. The way Noah looks at me tells me exactly where that is. He leans in, brushing his lips against mine gently. His mouth continues a path up my cheek, nipping his way up my neck until he gets to the spot behind my ear.

The spot. The one he knows will cause my legs to go all wobbly.

"In case you didn't know." He moves even closer now, his hands tracing the curve of my back before they wrap around me with tenderness and protectiveness. He slides a hand down the curve of my waist down to my thigh. He parts my legs, standing right in between them.

Noah winks at me, a mischievous glint in his eyes before his lips crash down on mine and we become lost in each other, in love.

Forever.

ACKNOWLEDGMENTS

Writing "IN CASE YOU DIDN'T KNOW" was incredibly difficult but I am so proud of it.

It's the culmination of months of research and writing amidst some of the toughest months of my life. Through the course of writing this novel; I've lost a few loved ones, gotten sick quite a few times and went through some of the worst bouts of depression and anxiety I have ever had.

Writing Ria and Noah's story helped me go on and kept me going. Even during the times when I couldn't see the end, I pushed through because I am so in love with their love that I knew I had to give it my all despite pouring from a nearly empty cup.

Why am I telling you this? Because I hope they can be there for you like they were for me.

I hope Ria inspires you with her resilience and strength.

I hope Noah encourages you to have faith and be patient through the tough moments.

I hope I did them justice and they help you believe again.

In life.

In the possibility of love.

In yourself.

There are quite a few people I need to thank but the person I want to thank the loudest is my husband. The man who inspired Noah (aka Agent *Thomas*).

Thank you for being my biggest cheerleader and my best friend. You have never wavered in your faith in me. In the darkest of times, you've held my hand and encouraged me, providing the light I needed to see past my deepest fears and insecurities. You believed in me when no one else did and provided me with the strength I desperately needed to keep moving forward and reach for a dream I thought was out of reach. Thank you for everything you do for our family. Thank you for this life we have. I love you.

To my daughter: Reach for the stars baby, over and beyond. Everything I do is to show you that no matter what life throws at you, you have it in you to come out better and stronger in the end. I love you to the moon and back.

To my sisters: Thank you for supporting me in this journey and for always having my back. I hope you see yourself in Ria and know you are just as resilient and strong as she is.

To Sierra Thomas; my editor, proofer and friend. Thank you for believing in "In Case You Didn't Know" and its potential. You took what I wrote and helped me turn it into something that I am so incredibly proud of. Thank you for sharing your brilliance and time but most importantly, I am so grateful for your trust and friendship. Because of you, this book is ten times better than it was. You are incredible.

To the amazing bookstagrammers who have cheered me on, sent me encouraging DMs, shared their platforms with me –– I cannot thank you all enough from the bottom of my heart and I truly hope I am not missing anyone here.

Thank you: Jessica, Julia, Missy, Min Young, Lopke, Kate, Mel, Nikki, Daisy, Gabby, Sam, Hannah, Erika, Caryl, Erica, Rachel, Tammy, Chandler, Val, Allie, Felicity, Penny, Allison, Beatriz, Emma, Gaby, Camille, Corey and to the many others across all social media platforms who have supported me from "Glad You Exist" to "In Case You Didn't Know."

You have no idea how much your messages and posts mean to me. There are simply no words sufficient enough to express my gratitude. You are amazing! Thank you!

To Authors Sonia Palermo, Nylah-Myesha, Torie Jean, K.H. Anastasia, Anna P, Maan Gabriel, Kristy Moore, Elicia Roper and Emma St. Clair; I can't even begin to describe how grateful I am to be surrounded by women who encourage and support one another in a world where we're conditioned to act the opposite. I am so in awe of your talent and grace. I hope you all know I am rooting for you just as proud and loud.

To Author Sarah Smith, I don't even know where to start when it comes to expressing my sheer appreciation for all the support and encouragement you've shown me. This time last year, I had just discovered your books and shyly DM-ing you about how much I loved the Filipino representation in them and now I get to shout you out in my own books, like what? You've inspired me so much and I'm truly honored and humbled that I get to call you my friend. *Maraming Salamat*!

Last, but not the least, I want to thank **you** for taking the time to read my novel.

My goal is to make you believe in the power of love and how it heals even the toughest of heartbreaks.

I hope you find solace and refuge in these pages and learn to love them as I do.

And remember, just like these characters, you matter.

You are worthy of your dreams.

You are worthy of love.

You are enough.

In Case You Didn't know, I'm glad YOU exist.

- Kaye Rockwell

Made in the USA
Middletown, DE
01 May 2022